Stacy th

Now, I'm not the ~~[obscured by barcode]~~
another person's d[obscured] just happened to be
open and I couldn't help seeing the entry
Amanda had made on Friday night.

It Said: *GREG AND JUDY MAKE ME
SICK. I WISH SOMEONE WOULD INTRO-
DUCE ME TO SOME INTERESTING BOYS!*

Someone? Hmmm . . . maybe there was a
way for me to make up to Amanda for the
problems she'd had with Greg.

Yeah, why not? Amanda would be really
pleased if I helped her find an interesting boyfriend. And it would be a good way of proving
to her that I wasn't as dumb as she thought.

Watch out, world: here comes Stacy the
Matchmaker!

Check out some of the other great books
in the Stacy and Friends series

1. The Great Sister War
2. Pippa's Problem Page
3. My Sister My Slave
4. My Real Best Friend

Stacy AND Friends

Stacy the Matchmaker

Allan Frewin Jones

Series created by Ben M. Baglio

RED FOX

A Red Fox Book
Published by Random House Children's Books
20 Vauxhall Bridge Road, London SW1V 2SA

A division of Random House UK Ltd
London Melbourne Sydney Auckland
Johannesburg and agencies throughout the world

Copyright © 1995 Ben M. Baglio and Allan Frewin Jones
Created by Ben M. Baglio

This edition 1998

1 3 5 7 9 10 8 6 4 2

First published in Great Britain by Red Fox 1995

The right of Allan Frewin Jones to be identified as the author of
this work has been asserted by him in accordance with the
Copyright, Designs and Patents Act, 1988.

Set in 12/14 Plantin by Intype, London

Printed and bound in Great Britain by
Cox & Wyman Ltd, Reading, Berkshire

RANDOM HOUSE UK Limited Reg. No. 954009

Papers used by Random House UK Limited
are natural, recyclable products made from wood grown in
sustainable forests. The manufacturing processes conform to
the environmental regulations of the country of origin.

ISBN 0 09 926363 7

Crash!

'Eyyow!' I yelled. It wasn't the noise of my sister Amanda slamming her bedroom door that made me yell. It was Benjamin, my cat. One second he was fast asleep on my legs; the next second there was this flurry of scrabbling claws and paws as he zipped under my bed.

My sister Amanda often has that effect. There are times when I feel like hiding under the bed myself to get away from her. Especially when she's in one of her moods. And judging by the way she'd just slammed her bedroom door, she was in a hurricane-alert, head-for-the-bomb-shelters, women-children-and-cats-first, mega-bad mood.

Bang!

That was Amanda's closet door. Her bedroom's right next to mine, so I get to hear all about it when Amanda's on the rampage.

I'd only been home from school for a half-hour. I was lying peacefully on my bed reading a book, with Benjamin dozing on my legs. I tipped myself over the edge of the bed and peered underneath. Benjamin stared out at me from the dark.

'It's OK,' I told him. 'She's not after you. You're perfectly safe.' I reached under the bed to give him a reassuring stroke.

Whack!

It sounded like she was kicking the furniture. Amanda only kicks the furniture when something really bad has happened. Like discovering a big red zit sitting on the end of her nose.

'I'd better go check what the problem is,' I told Benjamin, as I climbed off my bed. 'Before she demolishes the whole house.'

I went along the hall and listened at Amanda's bedroom door. *Thud!* I heard from inside. And then, 'Ow!'

'Everything OK in there?' I called.

'Ow! No!' Amanda yelled.

I opened the door and peeked in. Amanda was sitting on the bed clutching her foot. She scowled at me.

'What do you want, Stacy?' she said, rubbing her toes. That's me: Stacy Allen, ten years old, from Four Corners, Indiana.

'Oh, it's only you,' I said with a grin. 'I

thought a mad gorilla was on the loose in here.' I gave her a friendly smile.

'The only monkey around here is *you*!' Amanda snapped.

'Gorillas aren't monkeys,' I said. 'Gorillas are apes. I read it in a book. All monkeys have tails, but gorillas – '

'I don't care!' yelled Amanda.

'Tell me to mind my own business, if you like,' I said, 'but is something upsetting you?'

'I hurt my foot,' Amanda said.

'That's what happens when you kick the furniture,' I told her.

'Who asked you?'

'You're in a bad mood,' I said. 'I can tell.'

'Get lost!'

'Don't take it out on me,' I said. 'I'm only trying to be helpful. What happened?'

Amanda glared at me. 'Nothing happened. I can kick the furniture if I like. It's mine. I don't need permission from you to kick my own furniture.'

'Are you in trouble at school?' I asked.

This seemed the most likely explanation. Amanda is always getting into trouble with her teachers for forgetting homework and stuff like that. The only things Amanda really likes about school are gossiping with her friends and being head cheerleader. The rest is kind of beyond her.

'School? Huh!' Amanda said.

'Do you have a zit?'

'Get out of here!'

So it wasn't zits and it wasn't school. But something had happened. Even Amanda doesn't kick furniture for fun.

'Tell me,' I said. 'Maybe I can help.'

'Oh, sure,' Amanda said. 'I guess there's a whole bunch of stuff you can do to help me with *her*!'

Ha! Now we were getting somewhere. There was a 'her' involved.

'Did Cheryl say something?' I asked. Cheryl Ruddick was one of Amanda's Bimbo friends. I don't like Cheryl very much. If she was my friend she'd be annoying me all the time. Not that an airhead like Cheryl Ruddick would ever *be* my friend.

Amanda stared at me. 'What's Cheryl got to do with anything?' she asked.

'How should I know?' I said. 'You said *her*. I thought maybe – '

'I'm talking about Judy MacWilliams,' Amanda yelled.

Of course! Judy MacWilliams. Amanda's hate list goes something like this: 1. School work – 2. Chores around the house – and 3.

Judy MacWilliams. (I'm usually somewhere in Amanda's top ten hates, the same way she's usually in mine – but right then neither of us were at number 1.)

Amanda and Judy were, like, total rivals in their class. At this point I have to say that Amanda's kind of pretty – if you like blue-eyed bimbos with wavy blonde hair. Judy is pretty, too, with long glossy black hair and Barbie-doll looks. If our school held a Stuck-up Competition, I'm not sure who'd win – Judy or Amanda. But it would be *one* of them, that's for sure.

Amanda's last great triumph over Judy was when Judy got plaster of Paris all over her at Amanda's thirteenth birthday party, and left the house in disgrace. (I haven't got time to explain how that happened right now, but it was hysterical.) I hadn't heard much from Amanda about Judy since then, but judging from the expression on Amanda's face right now, Judy MacWilliams was right up there at the top of Amanda's hate list again.

'What did she do?' I asked. It was nice for Amanda to be angry with someone other than me for a change. I was dying to know what had happened.

'Nothing!' Amanda snapped.

'Nothing?' I said. 'She's got you this mad

by doing *nothing*?' Sheesh – what's it going to be like when Judy does *something*?

'She's just acting so *big*,' said Amanda. 'She thinks she's so smart. As if I care!' Amanda got up off the bed and stamped around the room. 'I don't care!' she yelled. 'I don't care *at all*!'

'Hey!' came Mom's voice up the stairs. 'What's all the noise? Are you two fighting again? I can hear you all the way down in the basement.'

I ran out of Amanda's room and hung over the banister.

'We're not fighting,' I called. 'Amanda's in a bad mood because of Judy MacWilliams. Even though Judy MacWilliams hasn't done anything. And Amanda says she doesn't care anyway.'

'I don't!' Amanda yelled, slamming her door behind me.

'Stacy, tell Amanda to keep the noise down,' Mom called. 'If she wakes Sam up I'll make sure she *does* care.'

'Mom?' I called softly.

'Yes?'

'You'll wake Sam up.'

Mom gave one of her growly 'Hmmms'.

I heard Amanda locking her door. Rats! She'd locked herself in there. *Now* how was I going to find out what Judy MacWilliams had done?

I guess I should explain a couple of things right now. You're probably wondering who Sam is, and why he shouldn't be woken up when it's only four o'clock in the afternoon.

Sam is my baby brother. He's only just over a year old, so he needs plenty of sleep. He's a real handful when he's awake, though, and he's the cutest thing you could imagine. He's got these big blue eyes and fluffy blond hair, and I just love him to pieces. He can almost walk, too, if you hold on to his hands, although he still falls over if you let go. And he's a lot better at crawling than he is at walking right now.

He sleeps in Mom and Dad's bedroom, but sometimes, when Mom is working down in the basement, she has him down there with her so she can keep an eye on him.

That's right, you read that right. My mom works in our basement. Dad converted it into a kind of office for her, so she could work from home. She works as a proofreader, which means she has the job of checking spelling and grammar in these huge books that arrive in the mail for her. Only they're not books yet, since they don't have covers or anything – not until Mom checks them at least. Anyway, it's really skilled work. I'm sure I couldn't do it, even though Ms Fenwick, my teacher, says my grammar is really good.

I've looked at some of my mom's manuscripts. They're full of words like 'gradation' and 'pecuniary'. I don't even know what 'pecuniary' means, so I'd *never* be able to figure out whether it was spelled right or not.

The other work my mom does is writing rhymes for greeting cards. Now, *that* I can understand.

Like this one she once wrote for a wedding card:

Something old and something new,
Something borrowed and something
blue,
But most of all, we wish for you,
A love that stays for ever true.

That is *so* sweet. My mom's really good at it. I wouldn't mind a job like that – writing happy messages for people to send to one another. Except that Mom says it's kind of hard to make a living doing it, which is why she does freelance proofreading, too.

My dad works as a travelling salesman. Selling books. He's not one of those guys who sticks his foot in your door and tries to get you to buy twenty-volume encyclopedias. He sells direct to bookstores. He works mostly in and around Chicago, which means that a lot of times he's away at night, because the town where we live isn't really all that close to Chicago. Sometimes, if he's really busy, we don't see him for days, which I don't really like.

I take after my dad in a lot of ways. He had crooked teeth when he was a kid, and I've got crooked teeth, too, which is why I have to wear a brace. Why me? When Amanda smiles, it's like you've lifted the lid off a piano keyboard. Gleam! Shine! My teeth gleam, too, but only because I've got a mouthful of metal.

Most people wouldn't think Amanda and I were sisters at all. There she is, all tall and graceful and blonde, and there's me, skinny and freckly with brown hair that doesn't have a single curl in it. Not that I'm jealous of how Amanda looks. Well, not *very* jealous. But it would be nice if I could find out what it would be like to be two years, six months, three days and six hours older than *Amanda*, instead of it being the other way around.

Then maybe I could behave toward *her* the same way *she* behaves toward *me*. I could treat her like a kid for a change. I think I'd enjoy that. Not that I would be anything nearly as big-headed and bossy as Amanda. At least, I hope not.

Anyway, as I was saying, Amanda had locked her door, which meant I wasn't going to find out any more for the time being, about what Judy MacWilliams had done.

I went back to my room. Still no sign of Benjamin.

I lay on the floor and peered under the bed. He was right at the back. I could see his eyes staring at me.

'Come on out, you big coward,' I told him.

He came slinking out and rubbed himself along my face, purring up a storm, his grey fur tickling my nose.

I sneezed. 'Look at you!' I said. 'All covered in dust.' I lifted him into my arms. 'You need a good brushing.'

Benjamin likes it when I brush him. I've got a special fine-toothed comb for him. I did his back, and then he rolled over like a big softie so I could comb his tummy.

'Our sister is in a bad mood,' I told him. 'And it has something to do with Judy MacWilliams.' Brush, brush. 'Amanda wouldn't tell me what it's all about. So you know what I'm going to do?' He stretched his chin out so I could carefully comb his neck.

'I'll tell you,' I said. 'Tomorrow at school,

I'm going to find out for myself what that nasty Judy MacWilliams has done.' I combed behind his ears. 'What do you think of *that*?'

I guessed from the volume of Benjamin's purrs that he agreed with me. After all, Amanda *is* my sister, even if she does drive me nuts at times. And when someone has upset my sister, it's my *duty* to try and fix things if I can.

Amanda and I both go to Four Corners Middle School, which is a short bus ride away from our house. I'm in sixth grade, and Amanda's in eighth grade, so we don't see a whole lot of each other during the day.

Unlike Amanda, I actually enjoy going to school. That's because I like learning new things. Amanda thinks she already knows everything. I guess her teachers don't agree with her, because she's always getting in trouble at home for her bad report cards.

In class, I sit next to Cindy Spiegel, who is my very best friend. Usually my other two best friends, Pippa Kane and Fern Kipsak, sit right behind us.

The four of us do everything together. And we always sit together in the cafeteria at lunch.

Today's big lunch news came from Cindy.

'Our house is being invaded,' she said, with this real gloomy look on her face. Cindy's not a naturally gloomy person. She's usually cheerful. She's very pretty, although, unlike Amanda, she doesn't make a big thing out of it. She's got naturally wavy auburn hair, and she was the first one of the four of us with pierced ears.

'Invaded?' Pippa said. 'By what? Cockroaches?' Pippa is the brains of our gang, I guess you'd say. Just don't ever ask her to do anything practical. She's kind of gangly and wears her long black hair in a braid down her back.

'No,' Cindy said. '*Worse* than cockroaches. We're being invaded by relatives. My uncle and aunt are coming to stay.' She gave us another gloomy look. 'Aunt Ruth and Uncle Timothy. And Luke's coming with them.' She sighed. 'Luke is such a nerd.'

I could just about remember Cindy's cousin Luke from two years back, when Cindy's mom had invited all her family over for a big Thanksgiving party. I only met Luke once. He wasn't what you'd call a very *memorable* person. In fact, all I could remember about him was that he refused to join in on any of the party games, and spent all the time staring at the TV and not talking to anyone. I guess he was around twelve at the time.

'What's so bad about that?' Fern asked. 'It's kind of fun when we have people to stay.'

17

'It would be OK if there was enough room,' Cindy said. 'But Mom's worked it out so that Aunt Ruth and Uncle Timothy get to sleep in *my* room. Which means I've got to sleep on the couch downstairs. For an entire week.'

'So where's Luke sleeping?' Pippa asked.

'In with Denny and Bob,' Cindy said. 'Everyone gets a bedroom except me.' Denny and Bob are Cindy's twin seven-year-old brothers.

'Maybe you could ask to swap with Luke?' Fern suggested with a grin. Fern has a really good sense of humour, and she's a lot of fun to be with, although if there's any trouble going on, you can be sure Fern will be right in there with it. She wears strange clothes, but that's because her parents are kind of hippies. Fern says she's just being an individualist. I admire that, but I still wouldn't go around in the things Fern likes to wear.

'What?' Cindy said, staring at Fern as if she'd just suggested she should bunk in with a couple of pigs. 'I'd rather sleep out in the *car*!'

'How long are they staying?' Fern asked.

'At least a week,' Cindy said.

'It's a strange time to take a vacation,' Pippa said.

'Oh, it's not a vacation,' Cindy told us.

'They sold their house in Lafayette and have bought a place in South Bend. It has something to do with Uncle Timothy's job. They're staying with us while the final arrangements are made.'

Lafayette is a big town south-east of Four Corners, and South Bend is way up north, near Lake Michigan. I guess it made sense for them to stay over in Four Corners. It made sense for *them*, I mean. It didn't make a whole lot of sense to Cindy right then.

'You mean they'll have all their furniture and everything with them?' Pippa said.

'No,' Cindy said. 'That's going up separately. I just hope it's not going to be *more* than a week. I know what it's going to be like. Denny and Bob will be acting up, like they always do when we've got visitors, and Luke will just sit in front of the TV the whole time. I won't get to watch anything I like, and I'm going to have to clear my stuff out of the living room every morning. It's going to be one big headache.'

'Hey,' I said. 'You could always stay over at my house until they go.'

Cindy shook her head. 'I already thought of that,' she said. 'Mom says I can't do that, because it'll seem as though I don't like them.'

'*Do* you like them?' Fern asked.

'Aunt Ruth and Uncle Timothy are fine,' Cindy said. 'But Luke is going to be a real pain.'

'Maybe he's changed for the better,' Pippa suggested, looking around at us. 'I mean, he'll be fourteen now, won't he? He could be completely different. When did you last see him?'

'Two years ago,' Cindy said miserably. 'And he's probably gotten even worse in the meantime. He'll probably be listening to heavy metal music and wearing T-shirts with skulls and crossbones on them. And I've got to be polite to him. Can you imagine it?'

I really sympathized with Cindy.

'He's probably one of these guys who leaves their dirty socks and stuff all over the house,' Fern said.

'Oh, thanks, Fern,' Cindy said. 'You really know how to cheer a girl up.'

'And you'll find horrible old slices of pizza stuffed down the back of the couch,' Fern said with a laugh. 'Fourteen-year-old boys are *always* leaving junk like that around for other people to clean up.'

'I'm so glad you told me that,' Cindy said miserably. 'That makes me feel *so* much better.'

'I'm only trying to help,' Fern said. 'You know, warn you of what to expect.'

'Well, you're *not* helping!' Cindy said. 'I don't want to be told how *bad* it's going to be. A person's friends are supposed to tell them that it'll be OK and that they shouldn't worry about it.'

'Cindy?' Fern said. 'Believe me: it'll be OK. Don't worry about it.'

'Huh!' Cindy snorted.

'When are they arriving?' Pippa asked.

'Friday,' Cindy said. 'And Dad's planning a barbecue for Sunday afternoon.' She looked around at us. 'Dad said it was OK for me to invite some friends.' She looked pointedly at Fern. 'Some *real* friends.'

'I *am* a real friend,' Fern said. 'Hey, come on, Luke will probably be out of the house most of the time. You'll probably hardly see him.' She smiled hopefully at Cindy. 'There, that's cheerful stuff. Do I get an invitation now?'

'Yeah,' Cindy said. 'You get an invitation. You're all invited. At least that's something for me to look forward to.'

Poor Cindy. From the look on her face right then, it was going to take a lot more than a barbecue to cheer her up.

21

* * *

I still had to get to the bottom of that business with Amanda and Judy MacWilliams.

It was time to go home and I was talking to my friends in front of the school. I'd told them about Amanda's bad mood the day before.

'Judy's probably showing off with some cool new clothes,' Cindy said.

'It's got to be something bigger than that,' I said. 'Something that would really drive Amanda wild. You should have heard her.'

'Hey,' Fern said. 'I think I might have the answer. Look!' She pointed out through the gates.

There were plenty of people standing around talking, but you couldn't miss Judy. For a start she had her horrible sidekick with her. Maddie Fischer. Maddie is kind of creepy. She follows Judy around like a pet dog. No, that's not fair. I like dogs. Maddie is more like a swamp-monster.

But it wasn't Maddie that caught our attention. It was the boy that Judy was talking to that we all looked at. He looked about fifteen, and even from that distance you could see Judy was showing off in front of him. I'll be honest with you: he was kind of cute, if you like boys. He had blond hair and a big denim jacket covered in buttons. There are quite a few boys like that around Four Corners, all looking like they think they're movie stars or something. But we didn't usually see them hanging around outside our school.

'Who is he?' Pippa asked.

'I don't know,' I said. 'I don't think I've ever seen him before.'

'He must be from the high school,' Cindy said.

'So what's he doing around here?' Pippa said.

Fern gave her a knowing look. 'What does it *look* like he's doing?' she said. 'He's here to see Judy.'

'Wow!' Pippa said. 'You mean – '

'Look!' Fern interrupted. 'He's taking her bag. And he's got his arm around her. They're *kissing*!'

They were, too. Right there in front of everyone.

We watched as Judy and the boy finished kissing. Then they walked off. Maddie followed behind them for a few steps, then Judy looked around at her and said something. Maddie came to a halt, her shoulders sort of sagging. Judy and the boy walked together along the pavement. Maddie stood looking at them for a few moments then wandered off on her own.

'Judy has a boyfriend,' I said, as the light dawned on me. 'That's what Amanda is so mad about! Judy MacWilliams has a boyfriend!'

3

After dinner that evening, Amanda and I were in the kitchen loading the dishwasher.

'Have you gotten over your bad mood?' I asked innocently. (She still didn't know that I'd seen Judy MacWilliams and *the boy.*)

'What bad mood?' Amanda asked. 'I don't have bad moods.'

'Are you nuts?' I said. 'You're one long bad mood. If they had classes in bad moods, you could be the teacher.'

Amanda tossed her hair. 'I don't know what you're talking about,' she said, handing me a plate. 'I'm the most even-tempered person I know.'

'Oh, right,' I said. 'So I *imagined* all that stuff last night?'

'I guess you must have,' Amanda said airily.

'So you're not mad at Judy MacWilliams any more?' I asked.

A sort of tremor went through Amanda,

not unlike a little earthquake. 'No,' she said, between her teeth.

'You're not *jealous* of her at all?'

Amanda gave a hard laugh. 'Me? Jealous of *her*? Are you kidding me? Why should I be jealous of Judy MacWilliams?'

I shrugged. 'Beats me,' I said. '*You* were the one kicking your furniture yesterday.'

'I was not. I was rearranging it, that's all.'

'With your feet?' I said.

Amanda just curled her lip. Well, if she wasn't going to admit her real feelings, I guess I was just going to have to prise them out of her.

'So,' I said, 'you aren't mad because Judy MacWilliams has a boyfriend, then?'

Amanda's lips tightened. She looked for a moment as if she planned on throwing a couple of plates across the room. 'What makes you think she's got a boyfriend?' Amanda said icily.

'Hasn't she?' I asked, innocent as a lamb. 'I kind of thought that guy who met her outside school might be her boyfriend?'

'What? Greg?' Amanda tossed her hair again. 'He's not her boyfriend.'

'It sure looked that way to me,' I said. 'They were kissing.'

'They were not!' Amanda said.

'They weren't?' I said. 'Gee, I wonder what they could have been doing then? It sure looked like a kiss to me.' Then it hit me. 'Hey, wait a minute,' I said. 'Did you say Greg? Didn't you want to date a guy called Greg a while ago?'

'I don't remember,' Amanda said.

'Sure you do,' I said. 'Greg Masterson. You can't fool me.'

It was all beginning to make sense now. Greg's sister Karen hangs out at the Happy Donut with Amanda and her friends. Amanda had been really mad when she'd missed a chance to meet him there a few weeks ago. (I guess I ought to admit that it was *my* fault she didn't get to meet up with him, but I don't have time right now to explain how it happened.)

No wonder Amanda was mad at Judy. Judy had snatched Greg right out from under Amanda's nose.

'Believe me,' Amanda said, 'Greg wouldn't go out with a jerk like Judy MacWilliams. He has more sense than that.'

'So what was he doing meeting her after school this afternoon?' I asked.

'Who knows?' Amanda said. 'Maybe he's started a charity that takes pity on losers.

Maybe she's just too dumb to find her own way home.'

'Get out of here,' I said. 'They were kissing. They're dating, *and* you know it. That's why you're so mad at her. Come on, Amanda, admit it.'

'If . . .' Amanda began, really icily. '. . . *If* Greg has gone out with Judy MacWilliams a couple of times, it's *only* because he's too nervous to ask out the person he really wants to date.'

'Run that one past me again?' I said.

Amanda gave me a cool smile. 'You don't know a thing about psychology,' she said. 'The fact is, Greg's scared to ask me out on a date.' She tossed her hair. 'He's afraid I might say no.'

'Let me get this straight,' I said. 'Greg really wants to date *you*?'

'Right,' Amanda said.

'But he's afraid *you* won't want to date *him*?'

'Right again,' Amanda said.

'Which is why he's dating Judy Mac-Williams instead of you?'

'You've got it,' Amanda said. 'The poor guy.'

'Amanda,' I said. 'You're crazy.'

'I wouldn't expect you to understand,'

Amanda said. 'I'm talking grown-up stuff, here.'

'I'll tell you what, Amanda,' I said. 'Why don't you go lie down in a darkened room for a while? Give your brain a rest. I think it's starting to overheat.'

Amanda gave me an angry look. 'Now look here, you little *kid*. If I wanted to date Greg, all I'd have to do is call him, right this minute. Judy MacWilliams? Huh! Greg wouldn't care less about Judy if he knew I was interested. And that's the truth.'

'So call him,' I said.

Amanda's face went kind of pale. 'What?'

'Call him,' I said. 'Ask him out, if you're so sure.'

'I don't have his number,' Amanda said.

'You do, too,' I said. 'You're always talking to his sister Karen on the phone.'

'He might not be in,' Amanda said.

'That's true,' I said. 'He might be out with Judy. I guess you'd better *not* call. You don't want to embarrass yourself.'

I grinned at Amanda. I'd never seen her like this before. Is *this* the effect boys have on you when you hit thirteen?

Amanda scowled at me. 'Do you think I'm chicken?' she said. 'Is that it?'

'I had kind of wondered where all the little yellow feathers were coming from.'

'OK!' Amanda said. 'That does it. I'll show you who's chicken, Stacy Allen. You can finish up in here on your own!' She threw some knives and forks into the dishwasher and marched out of the kitchen.

I watched her leave.

Wow! Did I hit a nerve!

I followed her into the hall. She was sitting on the stairs with the phone in her lap, punching the numbers. She glared at me as she put the receiver to her ear.

'Mrs Masterson?' she said. 'Hi, it's Amanda Allen. No, no, I don't want Karen. Could I speak to Greg, please?'

In the pause, she poked her tongue out at me. I jammed my fingers in the corners of my mouth and waggled my tongue right back at her.

'That's an improvement,' Amanda hissed at me. I heard a voice squawk through the receiver.

'Oh,' Amanda said into the phone. 'He isn't? No, it's nothing important. Could you just tell him that I called? No, no message. Thanks. Bye.' She slammed the phone down.

'Aww? Not in?' I said. 'Gee, I wonder *where* he could be?' I gave her a big grin. 'Maybe

Judy will be able to tell you at school tomorrow?'

Amanda lunged for me, but I managed to avoid her, zipping past her up the stairs.

I locked myself in my room, just for safety. When I get Amanda really mad, it's always a good idea to put a solid lump of wood between us.

* * *

I spent some time in my room colouring in a poster I'd bought in the mall a few days earlier. It was a big line-drawing of a whole bunch of butterflies that you could colour in yourself. I'd borrowed Amanda's magic markers and I'd already filled in three butterflies. One was red and blue, another was pink and pale green and orange; the biggest one of all was bright yellow. My favourite colour. When it was finished, I planned to pin it up over my bed.

I've got to admit, I'm not much of an artist. Amanda is the talented one in our family. She's brilliant at stuff like that. The best I can do is colour in posters that other people have drawn. Amanda's room is full of her own paintings and drawings. I guess it proves that you don't have to be smart to be artistic.

It was around eight o'clock when I heard the phone ring. I didn't pay any attention. If it was for me, someone would yell. But it wasn't. As usual, it was for Amanda. And she didn't waste any time coming up to my room and hammering on the door to tell me all about it.

'Hey, bean-brain,' she called. 'You still locked in there?'

She came in, her face almost split in two with this gigantic grin. 'That was Greg,' she said. 'Calling back.'

'Wow,' I said. 'So Greg knows how to use a phone, huh? You sure know how to pick them.'

'Don't you want to know what he wanted?' Amanda asked. It was obvious that she was dying to tell me.

'Not really,' I said.

'Well, I'll tell you anyway,' Amanda said in a irritating singsong voice. 'Just to prove to you that I was right all along and you were wrong.'

She flounced back to the door, tossing her hair. 'Greg just asked me out,' she said. 'So *ha*!'

She slammed the door behind her.

I ran to the door and yanked it open, yelling, 'I don't know what you're being so big-headed about. If it wasn't for me, you wouldn't have called him in the first place!'

'Stacy!' Dad hollered from downstairs. 'Keep the noise down, please.'

The last thing I saw of Amanda, before she danced into her room, was a big pink tongue.

Gee, wasn't Greg *lucky*? He was going out on a date with my totally mature sister. What a catch!

I went back into my room.

Now, I'm no expert on these things, but it did seem kind of strange to me that Greg would be walking Judy MacWilliams home one minute and then asking Amanda out the next.

Maybe Amanda had been right all along? Maybe all that stuff she'd been telling me in the kitchen wasn't as crazy as it had sounded.

Professor Von Allen of You-Figure-It-Out College, Indiana: *No, Stacy. Believe me, it was just as crazy as it sounded. Your sister is suffering from weird and twisted delusions brought about by too much hot air in her brain.*

Yes, that's just what I *thought*.

But it still didn't explain why Greg Masterson had asked her out on a date.

4

I was with Pippa and Fern in my room after school on Friday. Cindy couldn't come over because she had to go straight home to welcome her relatives. She wasn't looking forward to that, I can tell you.

'Don't you think you're overreacting a little?' I'd asked her over lunch. 'Anyone would think Luke was Count Dracula or something.'

'I wish he was,' Cindy had said. 'That way I could fill the house with garlic to ward him off. And Mom says I have to be nice to him. How can you be *nice* to a big fourteen-year-old nerd?'

'Don't panic,' Fern had told her. 'You'll end up a nervous wreck.'

End up? Cindy already *was* one.

I told the guys all about Amanda and the date she'd arranged with Greg. That was one of the reasons Pippa and Fern had come over. They wanted to be there when he picked her up. I mean, it was Amanda's first real date. We didn't want to miss out on seeing how she behaved when the big moment finally arrived.

Judging by the amount of time Amanda spent in the bathroom, she was going to a *lot* of trouble to impress Greg.

'Do you think boys spend as much time getting ready for dates as girls do?' Pippa wondered.

'No one in the entire world could spend as long as Amanda,' I said. 'She's been in there for over an hour.'

'She'll probably come out all wrinkled from the bath water,' Fern said. 'It'll be like dating a prune.'

We heard Amanda running up and down the hall. Every now and then she'd yell for Mom: 'Mom! I can't find my yellow hairband!' or 'Mom! One of the laces is broken!'

Fern lay back on my bed with her hands behind her head. 'Aren't you glad you don't want to date boys?' she said.

'You can say that again,' Pippa said. She looked at me. 'You know, you're kind of lucky, having a big sister like Amanda.'

'I am?' I said. 'How do you figure that out?'

'Well,' Pippa said. 'You get to see how dumb teenagers behave. You can look at Amanda and see what *not* to do when you're a teenager.

35

'I've been looking at Amanda and seeing what *not* to do for years,' I told her. 'I could write a book on it.'

The Stacy Allen Directory of Teenage Behaviour (with special thanks to Amanda Allen, without whom none of the dumb stuff in this book would have been written)

Chapter One: Dating Boys
Dating boys is no big problem for the sophisticated modern teenage girl. Just follow these simple steps for the perfect night out.

1. Call your intended date. Don't be put off by the fact that he's out with another girl. Remember: you're the most desirable girl in town. He's only out with another girl because he's too scared to call *you*.

2. Fix it so he takes you somewhere where you can really *shine*. Like the ice-rink. He can then spend the evening gazing at you in amazement as you do all those tricky moves out on the ice. You know, like the triple-axel and spin where you end up losing control and falling on your rear end. That's a real winner.

3. Preparations. This involves a whole

lot of running around. Go in and out of the bathroom at least five times an hour. Choose a whole set of your most flattering clothes. Run around a little more. Look at yourself in the mirror. Groan, because you think you look *awful*. Take off all your clothes and start again. (Do this at least three times.)

4. Sit around looking real jumpy and nervous. Calm yourself down with a chocolate shake. Spill the shake down your front and dash up to your room to find a new top.

5. Jump right out of your *skin* when the doorbell rings. Run upstairs screaming when you yank the door open and find that it's only Pippa.

6. PANIC!

I'd managed to get a few more details of the date out of Amanda. The plan was, Greg was going to pick her up at six o'clock, and they'd go to the Paradice ice-skating rink together. Although, by the way Amanda was racing around the house in a total frenzy, you'd think he'd invited her to meet the President or something.

I looked at the clock. It was five to six.

'Let's go downstairs,' I said. 'We'll get to see the whole thing from the living room.'

We trooped downstairs. Dad wasn't home yet, and Mom was doing something in the kitchen. The three of us sat in a row on the couch, just waiting for the doorbell to ring.

Amanda came flying in. She had on her best black jeans, and a white satin top. She'd obviously spent ages getting her hair right, and she even had some make-up on.

She went straight over to the window without even noticing us.

'You've got baby powder on your rear end,' I told her. She twisted around, trying to see the smudge. 'Arrgh!' she yelled, running out again. 'Mom! I need a cloth!'

We looked at each other and grinned. Another handy tip for Chapter One of my book: *Don't sit in the baby powder.*

'Your sister is crazy,' Fern said.

'Tell me about it,' I said.

Pippa got up and walked over to the window. It was exactly six o'clock. 'Uh-oh!'

'Is he here?' I asked.

'UH-OH!' Pippa said again. She looked around at us and waved us over. 'You guys have *got* to see this.'

I looked out of the window.

'Wow!' Fern breathed over my shoulder. 'This is going to be like World War Three!'

It was Greg. But it wasn't *only* Greg. Someone else was with him.

'Oh, my gosh!' I said. 'I've got to warn Amanda!'

I ran out of the living room in time to see Amanda disappearing upstairs. I raced after her, and caught up with her just as she was picking up her bag from her room.

'Is he here?' she asked. She looked really nervous. 'Do I look OK?'

'Yes, you look fine,' I said. 'But there's something I've got to tell you.'

Amanda pushed past me. 'Not now, Stacy.'

'You're really going to *want* to know this,' I said.

'Later!' Amanda snapped.

I grabbed her arm. '*No*! Not later. Right now! He's got someone with him!'

Amanda stared at me as if I'd just spoken to her in a foreign language. 'What do you mean?'

'I mean he's not alone,' I said, then took a deep breath. 'He's with Judy.'

'Whaaat?' Amanda yelled.

'They're coming up the driveway – together!' I said.

Amanda was still staring blankly at me when

the doorbell rang. 'It's not true,' she said. 'You're kidding me?' She grabbed me by the shoulders and shook me. 'Tell me you're kidding me!'

'It's true!' I said.

For a moment I thought she was going to scream. Then she gave me a really miserable look. 'True?'

I nodded.

She let go of me. 'Calm!' she said, closing her eyes. 'I've got to be calm!'

Now, you've probably noticed I don't often say much in praise of Amanda. But I was really impressed how she behaved right then.

She took a couple of deep breaths, fixed this big smile on her face, then walked down the stairs as if nothing bad had happened.

'Hi, Greg,' she said, opening the front door. 'Hi, Judy.'

'Are you ready?' Greg asked.

'Just about,' Amanda said. 'I just have to go get my bag.' She came running back up the stairs. She had a look on her face that would blister paint.

I handed her bag to her. She grabbed me around the neck with both hands, giving me this real evil glare as she pretended to strangle me.

'That's what I'd like to do to her,' she hissed.

Phew! I was real glad I wasn't Judy when I saw the look in Amanda's eyes.

She let go of me and fixed the grin back in place.

'Uh . . . have a nice time,' I said cautiously.

She didn't say anything else. She just walked back down the stairs and out.

I ran down to the others.

We just looked at one another. There's not a lot you can say when your big sister's first date turns up with another girl.

'I've said it before, and I'll say it again,' Fern said. 'Aren't you glad you don't want to go out with boys?'

* * *

I was lying on the couch in the living room, my head on the arm and my legs stretched out over Dad's lap. My dad is a very comfortable person to lie all over. He soon lets me know when he gets sick of being used as a cushion. First he'll give me a quick tickle just under my ribs. A sort of cautionary tickle, to let me know I should be moving. And if that doesn't work, he really goes to town, and I end up as a screaming, blubbering wreck on the living-room carpet.

Right then, he was reading a magazine that he rested on my legs.

'Dad?' I asked. 'Why don't I want to date boys?'

He looked at me. 'Do you *want* to want to date boys?' he asked.

'No way,' I said. 'I just wondered why I don't.'

'I guess it's because you've got better things to do,' Dad said. That was true. I had several *million* better things to do. But it didn't really answer the question.

'But I guess I *will* want to when I'm older?' I asked.

'I guess so,' Dad said.

'So what happens?' I asked. 'Am I going to wake up one morning and think, hey, I want to go out with boys?'

'I'll tell you the truth, honey,' Dad said. 'I really don't remember *how* it happens.' He looked across at Mom, who was in the armchair working on her needlepoint. 'Do you remember how you started getting interested in boys?' he asked her.

'I remember thinking they were scary,' Mom said. 'And I remember being scared half to death on my first date.' She shrugged. 'But I guess it's like anything else; once you get used to the idea, you get to like it.' She smiled at me.

I looked at her. 'I don't think boys are scary,' I said. 'I just think they're boring.'

Mom nodded. 'That's fine,' she said. 'You keep on thinking that and you'll save yourself a lot of trouble.'

Someone opened and closed the front door real quiet. It had to be Amanda, although she usually comes in and out of the house like a major landslide. She'd been gone a couple of hours.

'Hi, honey,' Mom called. 'You're back early. Did you have a nice time?'

I heard Amanda take a couple of steps up the stairs before she came back down and stood in the living-room doorway. She looked real miserable.

'No,' she said. 'I did *not* have a nice time. I had a totally horrible time. I know he *won't*, but *if* Greg Masterson calls, I'm not in. Never. Ever!'

Dad gave her an anxious look.

'Do you want to tell us about it?' he asked.

'No. I never want to hear Greg Masterson's name mentioned in this house again.'

Well, no problem there. Apart from Amanda, no one ever mentioned Greg anyway.

She went up to her room.

Mom sighed. 'There you go, Stacy,' she

said. 'That's what happens when you start wanting to date boys.'

I gave Amanda a little while to recover, then went up to find out what had happened.

Newsflash! Thirteen-year-old schoolgirl Judy MacWilliams was found murdered at the Paradice Ice Rink this evening. Witnesses who found the body say she looked like she'd been run over at least twenty times by someone wearing ice-skates. Police are looking for a blonde teenager with an angry expression.

I stuck my head around Amanda's door. She was sitting at her desk, staring into space with her chin in her hands.

'How'd it go?' I asked.

She looked slowly around at me. 'How did it go?' she said. 'How did it *go*? How do you *think* it went, you dumb, freckle-faced, metal-mouthed moron?'

'Hey, don't take it out on me,' I said.

'Why not?' Amanda said. 'The whole thing was your fault in the first place. I've just spent a night of total humiliation because of you!'

I gaped at her. 'Me?' I said. 'Why, what did I do?'

'You got me to call him,' she said.

'But you said – '

'Get out!' Amanda yelled. 'Just get out and leave me alone.'

I got out. Sheesh! What a grouch.

I thought I'd been doing her a favour. Amanda was the one who was desperate to date Greg. All I did was give her a little push in the right direction.

Had I *forced* her to call Greg? Had I fixed it so he'd turn up with Judy MacWilliams? I certainly hadn't. But the way Amanda was behaving, it looked like I was going to get all the blame for it.

Well, I got that right. The next morning she was like a porcupine with a sore throat that had sat on a cactus. I'd obviously gone all the way to the top of Amanda's hate list.

She came storming into my room on Saturday morning; at the crack of *dawn* almost. Benjamin was under the bed before you could say 'dogs'. 'Do you have my magic markers?' she yelled.

I didn't even look out from under my blankets. 'Over there,' I said, waving my arm toward my desk.

Stamp, stamp, stamp. Over to the desk. 'I wish you wouldn't just *take* my things,' Amanda said.

'You lent them to me,' I reminded her, from under the covers. 'So I could colour my poster.'

'Yeah,' Amanda said. '*Weeks* ago.'

'Two days ago,' I corrected her.

'That's not the *point*,' Amanda said. 'You should learn to give things back.'

She went stamping out. I turned over and went back to sleep.

'Stacy!' I was reawoken by another yell in my ear.

I floundered under the covers. 'Now what?'

'Have you been using my shampoo?' Amanda was in her robe, wet hair dripping all over.

'No, I haven't.'

'*Someone* has.'

I sat up, giving her a look like she'd just told me the house had been burgled. 'Oh, no!' I said. 'Someone's used your special *shampoo*? What are we going to *do*, Amanda? Do you think we should call the cops?'

'Very funny, Stacy.'

'Maybe we should get the Feds in?' I made a noise like a police siren and cupped my hands over my mouth so my voice sounded like a radio message. 'Calling all cars. Calling all cars. Be on the lookout for a dangerous shampoo thief. Description: the thief will have shiny, manageable hair and not a single split end.'

Amanda glared at me and stormed out.

'*Mom* used your shampoo,' I called after her. 'Go arrest *her*!

47

The first thing I did after I got up was to have a good look around my room for anything else I'd borrowed from Amanda and forgotten to give back. Then I took all the stuff and dumped it outside her bedroom door.

If she was going to insist on being mad at me because she had a bad time with Greg Masterson, then the fewer reasons she had to yell at me the better.

I was down in the kitchen fixing myself some breakfast when I heard her tripping over the stuff as she came out of her bedroom.

You'd think people would watch where they were going.

I didn't wait for her to come down and carry on blaming me for everything that had ever gone wrong in her life. I just grabbed a slice of toast and got out of there.

Actually, I felt kind of honour-bound to go visit Cindy. I thought she could use some moral support over there.

I was just crossing the street when a brown-haired head bobbed up over the wall of the Browns' house.

'Hi!'

'Hi, Davey,' I said. The Browns had moved in opposite us a couple of years ago. Davey is a year younger than me. I never pay much attention to him, to tell the truth. He is one of those people who seem to spend an awful lot of time on their own. My Mom says it's because he's an only child. I don't know about that, but he is kind of strange.

'You going someplace?' he asked, climbing up on to the wall and swinging his legs, his head tipped to one side like a bird watching for a worm.

'A friend's house,' I told him. I was a little surprised. Davey isn't exactly the sort of person you have chats with.

He didn't say anything else. He just sat there looking at me.

'I'd better be going,' I said.

'My Mom's baking chocolate cookies,' he said.

'That's nice,' I answered.

'Do you want some?' he asked.

'Not right now, thanks,' I said. 'I just had breakfast.'

'Another time, huh?' he said.

'Sure. Bye.'

I headed off, but when I reached the corner, I glanced around. He was still sitting there, staring at me.

That Davey Brown is one strange boy.

Cindy lives only a few blocks away. When I got to her house, I was half-expecting there'd be some kind of sign to show her relatives were there. You know, like the house walls bulging out to fit them all in. But the only obvious thing was a second car in the driveway.

Inside the house, things were pretty chaotic. Cindy had only just let me in when Denny and Bob came screaming down the stairs, yelling at the tops of their voices and zapping with ray guns. Luke raced down after them.

I recognized him right away, although he was a lot taller and bigger than I remembered. He still had his hair all falling in his eyes. But the way he was behaving was completely different from how I remembered him.

Like I told you, two years ago Luke had spent all his time staring at the TV screen and ignoring everyone. The Luke that came racing down after Cindy's brothers didn't seem like the same person at all. He was smiling and laughing. Boy, two years had sure made a big difference to him.

He came to a skidding halt at the foot of the stairs and grinned at me.

'This is Stacy,' Cindy said, above the noise her brothers were making.

'Yeah, I remember,' Luke said. 'How's it going, Stacy?'

'Fine,' I said, in surprise.

'Can't stop now,' he said. 'I've got Martian invaders to catch.'

He chased them down the hall, Denny and Bob yelling and zapping and falling over each other to get away from him.

'Can we go to Pippa's house?' Cindy said. 'I'd kind of like some peace and quiet for a while.'

We headed off to where Pippa lived.

'How's it been?' I asked, as we walked along.

'Actually, it's been OK,' Cindy said. 'You wouldn't believe how different Luke is. He's changed completely. He was real friendly right from the start. I was expecting him to be a total monster, but he's very nice.'

'I guess he's grown up a little,' I said.

'A *lot*,' Cindy agreed.

'So you think it's going to be OK, having them stay?' I asked.

'It looks that way,' Cindy said. 'Apart from the fact that I've got to sleep on the couch, I think everything's going to be fine.'

'I'm glad *someone*'s happy,' I said.

'Why? What's wrong?' Cindy asked.

I filled her in on what had happened the night before.

'Amanda must have been so embarrassed,' Cindy said. 'And Judy MacWilliams, of all people. Amanda must really hate her.'

'I don't know about that,' I said. 'Amanda's

51

blaming me right now. She says it's all my fault.'

Pippa lives alone with her mom in a real neat little house full of books. Pippa's mom is a college professor. I guess that's where Pippa gets her brains from.

When we arrived, Pippa's mom was under their car doing some kind of repair work on it. Mrs Kane is practical like that. I guess you have to be, if you're a woman living on your own. Pippa might have inherited her brains from her mom, but she sure didn't get any of her mom's other skills. She's the kind of girl who can't put a plug in a socket without blowing every fuse in the house.

Mrs Kane said we could go right in. Pippa was in their living room watching some educational programme on TV.

Cindy switched over to some cartoons while Pippa got us a Coke from the fridge.

'I guess Amanda's got a point,' Pippa said, after I'd told her how Amanda was behaving toward me. 'If you hadn't made fun of her, she wouldn't have called Greg.'

'I wasn't making fun of her. I was trying to help her out. She said she'd only have to snap her fingers and he'd come running.'

'I guess that's right,' Pippa said. 'How were

you supposed to know that Greg would turn up with Judy?'

'Exactly,' I said. 'But how do I get Amanda to see it that way?'

'What you need to do, Pippa said, 'is come up with some plan to get Greg and Amanda together, right? That way you'll make everything all right, and Amanda won't be mad at you any more.'

'And how exactly am I going to do that?' I asked.

'Why not invite them both to Cindy's barbecue?' Pippa said. She looked at Cindy. 'Do you think your folks would mind if a few extra people show up?'

'I guess not,' Cindy said. 'So long as I warned them in advance. But what good would that do? Greg would just show up with Judy again.'

Pippa grinned. 'Yeah,' she said. 'But *we'd* be there.'

'Oh, right,' I said. 'I get it. We kidnap Judy and lock her in the garage. Cute idea, Pippa. One of your *best*.'

'Are you telling me', Pippa said, 'that the four of us can't come up with some way of getting Judy away from Greg long enough for Amanda to move in on him?'

I looked at them. Cindy looked unsure, but Pippa gave me a big grin.

'There's just one problem with this plan,' I said.

'What's that?' Pippa asked.

'*You* thought of it,' I said. Cindy nodded in agreement. If there was one thing we both knew from experience, it was that Pippa's brilliant plans *always* went wrong.

Pippa looked kind of hurt. 'Oh, fine,' she said. 'Forget it, then. I thought you were looking for a way of getting Amanda off your back. Maybe you should come up with your own plan.'

Cindy and I looked at each other.

'What do you think?' I asked Cindy.

'Do you have a better idea?' Cindy asked me.

'I guess not.'

'What could go wrong?' Pippa said.

I looked at her. *Plenty*, I thought. But on the other hand, I wasn't exactly full of brilliant ideas myself. 'Oh, heck,' I said. 'Let's do it.'

I guess I'm just gullible like that. No matter how many times Pippa's grand schemes went wrong, there was always the hope in the back of my mind that *this* time, just this *once*, things might go the way we planned.

6

The first thing we needed to do was check with Cindy's folks that it was OK to invite a bunch more people to the barbecue. There was no way Amanda would be interested in coming unless she could bring some of her friends.

No problem there.

'Why not?' Mr Spiegel said, when we went to Cindy's house to ask. 'The more the merrier, huh?'

'I knew Dad would go for it,' Cindy told us afterward. 'He just loves showing off with the barbecue.'

My next task was a little trickier.

Amanda was in the living room when I got home. She'd pushed the couch back and was on the rug, in front of one of her exercise videos. She was stretched out on her back with her hands behind her head, lifting her shoulders off the rug in time to some disco music. On the screen a woman in a leotard was doing the same thing. '*Hup! Hah! Hup! Hah!*' Amanda panted as she jerked her shoulders up and down.

'Hey, Amanda?' I yelled above the music.

'*Hup! Hah!* Get lost, Stacy. *Hup! Hah!*' *Hup* when she went up, *hah* when she came down.

'Do you want to come to a barbecue at Cindy's house?' I shouted.

'*Hup!* No! *Hup!* I! *Hup!* Don't!'

'You can invite some friends,' I yelled. (I've never really figured out why exercise music has to be so *loud*.)

Amanda stopped jerking up and down and gave me a sour look.

'I don't want to go to any dumb barbecue at Cindy's house,' she said.

'It'll be great,' I said. 'It'll cheer you up.'

She glared at me. 'Do I look like I need cheering up?' she said.

'I thought you might still be a little down about last night,' I said. 'I'm only trying to be nice.'

'Don't bother,' Amanda said.

I put on my most sympathetic face. 'Was it really bad?' I asked.

Amanda sat up. 'Bad?' she said. 'You mean was it bad that the guy you talked me into asking on a date turned up with his *girlfriend*?'

'Hey, come on now,' I said. 'You were the

56

one who said Greg really wanted to go out with you.'

'Can I help it if he's too dumb to *know* what he really wants?' Amanda said. She looked at the TV and started doing some twisting and stretching moves along with the woman in the leotard. 'Anyway,' she said, 'like I told you last night – I don't want to hear his name mentioned in front of me ever again. Got me?'

'If you say so,' I said. I wasn't going to be put off that easily. Amanda could pretend she wasn't interested in Greg any more – but I knew better.

'But what about this barbecue?' I asked. 'It's tomorrow afternoon.'

'Who's going?'

'Plenty of people,' I said. 'Cindy's folks will be there. And her aunt and uncle and cousin. And me, and Fern and Pippa.'

'Wow!' Amanda said. 'It sounds like a real wild party. I'm not sure I'd be able to cope with the excitement, Stacy.'

'I told you,' I said. '*You* can invite some people, too.'

'Forget it,' Amanda said. 'I'm not interested.' She pressed the volume button on the remote control so the music got too loud for me to shout over.

Rats! Now what was I going to do?

I went into the kitchen, poured myself a glass of milk and raided the cookie jar. Cookies are real brain food, you know. Whenever I can't think of a solution to a problem, I always find that eating a couple of cookies helps.

Cookies, and How They Help.
The Stacy Allen Guidebook

One Cookie: For simple stuff, like helping you remember where you put your gym socks.

Two Cookies: Slightly bigger problems. Like explaining to Mom how you got jelly down inside the toaster.

Three Cookies: Even *bigger* problems. This covers everything from maths homework to covering up for Benjamin clawing the couch.

Four Cookies: Mega-big problems. Like fixing it so Amanda meets up with Greg at Cindy's barbecue.

Five Cookies. Whoo! World peace and a three-month trip to Disneyland!

I was just helping myself to cookie number four when the phone rang. Mom and Dad were out shopping with Sam. Otherwise Amanda would never have been allowed to have her music on that loud. I let it ring a few times. In this house about ninety per cent of the calls are for Amanda.

I let it ring six times before I went to answer it. Sure enough, it was for Amanda. It was Rachel Goldstein, one of her Bimbo pals; the dumbest girl in the whole school.

'Hey, Stacy,' she said. 'Get Amanda for me.'

This is a perfect example of how Amanda's friends treat me. Like they'd probably *die* if they had to say *please*.

I was just about to put the phone down and yell for Amanda when the cookies started working. Brainwave! 'I hope the weather's good for the barbecue tomorrow,' I said.

There was a long silence on the other end of the phone.

'Hello?' I said. 'Anyone the-ere?'

'What barbecue?' Rachel asked.

'The one at the Spiegels' house. Hasn't Amanda called you about it yet? I told her she could invite a few friends.'

'She hasn't said anything to me,' Rachel said.

'Huh!' I said. 'That's Amanda!'

'Is she there?' Rachel asked. 'Can I speak to her?'

'Hold on,' I said. I put the phone down and stared up and down the hall. 'Hello, Rachel?' I said, picking the phone up again. 'I looked for her, but can't see her. My folks are out shopping. Maybe Amanda went with them.'

Did I lie to her? Not really. I *did* look for Amanda, and I sure didn't see her anywhere in the hall. And Mom and Dad *were* out shopping. And Amanda *could* have gone with them. She *hadn't*, but she *could* have.

'So what's the deal with this barbecue?' Rachel asked.

I gave her a quick run-down of the time and address. 'Hey,' I said. 'If Amanda's out shopping she might not have had time to call anyone yet. Maybe you could call a few people and tell them. Just in case.'

'Yeah, OK,' Rachel said.

'Don't forget to call Karen Masterson,' I said. I crossed my fingers, because I was about to come out with a little white lie. 'And tell Karen to invite her brother, Greg. I know Amanda was going to ask both of them.'

'OK,' Rachel said. 'But you tell Amanda she can do her *own* inviting in the future. What am I, her secretary?'

'You know Amanda,' I said.

I put the phone down and did a little victory dance around the hall. Sometimes I'm so smart I *amaze* myself.

You're probably thinking, but, hey, Amanda said she didn't want to go. That's because you don't know how the Bimbos operate. (We call Amanda and her gang of friends the Bimbos. They call me and my pals the Nerds. The difference is that they *are* bimbos, and we're *not* nerds.)

I reckoned it would be about a half-hour before one of the Bimbos phoned back, wanting to chat with Amanda about what they should all wear, and what time to arrive. Then Amanda could hardly tell them she wasn't going, could she?

My guess was that it would be Cheryl who phoned first.

I'm telling you. A half-hour, tops.

* * *

I was wrong. About the time, anyway.

The phone rang about ten minutes later. It was Cheryl.

I yelled for Amanda then put the receiver down and went upstairs, so I could listen in without Amanda seeing me.

'Hi,' I heard Amanda say. 'I was just doing my exercises. I've got this great new video.' There was a pause. 'Huh?' Pause. 'Rachel?' Pause. 'She did?' A longer pause. 'Yeah, I *knew* about it, but –'

I peeped around the banister. Amanda was standing there looking real perplexed. 'I

61

wasn't going to bother,' Amanda said. 'It sounded really boring. OK, OK, if everyone else is going, I guess I will, too.'

Yesss! That was all I needed to hear. Step 1 of the Great Matchmaking Plan was in place.

The Great Matchmaking Plan
Step 1. Get Amanda and Greg to the barbecue.
Step 2. Get rid of Judy.
Step 3. Get Amanda and Greg together.
Step 4. Amanda and Greg start dating. Amanda is in a permanent good mood and I don't get yelled at any more.
I have to admit, there were a couple more Steps in my mind as well . . .
Step 5. I tell Amanda all about Steps 1 through 4.
Step 6. Amanda realizes how much I've helped her, and finally stops treating me like a dumb kid.

I was still basking in the success of Step 1 when, fifteen minutes later, Amanda came into my room.

'What are you up to?' she asked. 'How did Cheryl know about that barbecue?'

'Someone must have told her,' I said.

'I know *that*,' Amanda said. 'You did!'

'I did not,' I said. 'I told Rachel.'

'Why?'

I gave her a hopeful smile. 'I'm only trying to make up for getting you into that mess with . . . uh . . . *him*,' I said. (Remember, I wasn't supposed to mention Greg's name in front of Amanda ever again.) 'I thought if you went to the barbecue, it'd cheer you up a little.'

'I told you I didn't want to go,' Amanda said.

'Yeah, I know,' I said. 'But I knew you'd have a good time once you were there. Sometimes people need a little push to get them to do something they'd enjoy.' I gave her my friendliest smile. 'I was only thinking of you, Amanda.'

She frowned at me. 'OK,' she said. 'I guess you thought you were doing me a favour.'

'So you're going?' I asked.

She shrugged. 'I guess so. But not because you cornered me into it, Stacy. I'm going because I changed my mind, all right? Don't you go thinking you can run my life for me.'

'Would I do that?' I said.

She gave me a sideways look. I could see she hadn't completely swallowed my story.

'It'll be fun,' I said. 'You'll see. You'll have a great time.'

At least, I hoped she would. It all depended

now on Steps 2 through 4 working out the way I'd planned.

Fingers crossed. And toes crossed, too. And *eyes* crossed. In fact, I crossed *everything*. I hadn't forgotten that this was all Pippa's idea, so *anything* could happen.

7

Hi, folks, this is Stacy Allen, your society reporter, speaking to you from one of this season's main events. It's a sunny Sunday afternoon in Four Corners, Indiana. Temperatures are up in the seventies and we look set for a great afternoon's entertainment. Mr Spiegel has managed to light the barbecue on his fourth attempt and there's a whole lot of food just waiting for its turn to burn.

The guests are starting to gather, and you can see from the look of anticipation on their faces that they're expecting a real bonanza show. Over on the patio Mrs Spiegel and her sister Ruth are laying out some salads. And here comes Ruth's husband and their son, Luke, to put some more cans in the cooler.

I arrived early to help set up the tables and chairs, and to spread out a few blankets on the lawn. The stereo was on a chair just outside the patio doors, so we could have some music.

Fern and Pippa arrived soon after me and, as soon as all the preparations were finished, the four of us got into a huddle to discuss Step 2 of our plan – how to get rid of Judy MacWilliams.

'You know, Greg might not come with Judy at all,' Pippa said. 'He might just arrive with Karen.'

'That would be perfect,' I said. 'But we can't *rely* on that happening. We've got to think how to get rid of Judy, just in case.'

'I've got it,' Fern said. 'If Greg arrives with Judy, we tell her there's been a call from home, and that she's got to go straight back.'

'A call saying what?' Cindy asked.

'Her house is on fire?' Fern suggested.

'Isn't that a little drastic?' I asked.

'OK,' Fern said. 'We'll say that just one room in her house is on fire. Her bedroom?'

'I don't really think so,' Pippa said. 'Could we come up with some *sensible* suggestions please, guys?'

'OK,' Fern said. 'If you don't go for the fire idea, how about we wait until Judy needs to use the bathroom, and then lock her in there?'

'And what if someone else needs to use it?' Cindy asked.

'You can tell them the bathroom is out of order,' Fern said.

Pippa sighed. 'And this is you being *sensible*, huh?'

'I think I've got it,' I said. 'What if Judy got something spilled down herself? She'd have to go off and clean up. And while she was doing that, we could make sure Amanda and Greg get together.'

'Not bad,' Pippa said. 'A nice juicy chicken leg down the front of her clothes. That would keep her busy for a while.'

'OK,' Cindy said. 'How do we do it?'

'Easy,' Pippa said. 'One of us accidentally bumps into her, or trips, or something, and – *kersplat!*'

'So,' Fern said, 'what we're looking for is someone to volunteer for a suicide mission, right? I mean, Judy is going to go crazy. She'll definitely *kill* whoever volunteers.'

'It's Cindy's house,' I said quickly. 'I think she should do it.'

'No, thank *you*,' Cindy said. 'This whole thing is Pippa's plan. She should do it.'

'No way,' Pippa said. 'It's Stacy's sister we're trying to help.' All three of them looked straight at me. 'So it's up to Stacy to get Judy out of the picture.'

You know, I *thought* they were going to say that.

67

'Couldn't we draw straws or something?' I said. 'I mean, be democratic about it.'

'OK,' Pippa said. 'Hands up all those who think Stacy should do it.' Three hands went up.

'Hands up all those who think Stacy *shouldn't* do it,' I said. I put both my hands up.

'Cheat,' Fern said. 'And you're still outvoted.'

'That's decided, then,' Pippa said. 'Stacy spills some food on Judy. Then you, Cindy, can go over to her and say something like, "Gee, you'd better come into the bathroom and wipe that off." Then you take her inside and keep her busy for as long as you can.'

'And while they're inside,' I said, 'we make sure Amanda and Greg get together.'

'Should we have a backup plan in case it goes wrong?' Fern suggested.

Pippa gave her a real superior look. 'What could possible go wrong?' she said.

That was exactly what was worrying me. I had a horrible feeling *plenty* could go wrong.

* * *

A few more people arrived: some grown-up neighbours of Cindy's parents who mostly stood around chatting on the patio and

68

drinking beer. The first batch of food was ready by then, and we went up with our paper plates to get some.

The twins, Denny and Bob, had a few friends over as well, and they took over the far end of the yard, yelling and running around and falling over one another the way seven-year-old boys always do.

Luke was helping Mr Spiegel out with the barbecue. 'Hi, Stacy,' he said, when we went over to get ourselves some drinks. 'What would you like?'

'Coke, please,' I said.

He opened the cooler. 'One Coke coming right up,' he said with a grin. He was wearing shades and a T-shirt with 'Lafayette Ice-World' printed on it. Two years ago he'd been kind of skinny and weedy, but now I had the chance to look at him again, I could see that he was a lot more healthy-looking.

'Whoo,' Fern whispered in my ear. 'Hot!'

'Sshh!' I hissed back at her. Fern can be real embarrassing sometimes. She doesn't care what she says.

Luke smiled at her.

Fern grinned right back at him. 'Cindy told us you were some kind of total slob last time she met you,' she said.

'Fern!' Cindy yelled, going bright red. 'I didn't!'

'Yes you did,' Fern said. 'You told us he spent all his time in front of the TV.'

Luke laughed. 'That was a while ago,' he said. 'I guess I was a real pain last time we were over here.' He looked at Cindy. 'Two years is a long time. And I *was* pretty slobby then, wasn't I?'

Cindy was too embarrassed to say anything. She just took a can and headed back to our blanket.

We followed Cindy down the yard.

'Why did you tell him that!' Cindy hissed at Fern.

'Hey, what's the problem?' Fern asked. 'He didn't mind. Was he a slob or wasn't he?'

'He isn't now,' Cindy said. 'He's real nice now.'

'Mm,' Fern said. 'And cute, too.'

I looked back at Luke. I guess he was kind of nice-looking. 'Hey, Fern likes Luke,' I said. 'Do you want us to fix up a date, Fern?'

We giggled as Fern made a face. The idea of her going on a date with Luke was pretty funny.

'So where's Amanda?' Pippa asked a while later. 'And Greg?'

'Amanda always shows up late,' I said. 'She

likes to make a big entrance once everyone else has arrived.'

'Well, here comes Greg,' Cindy said. We looked around. Greg and Karen and Judy were just coming down the side of the house.

'Darn!' I said. 'He brought Judy.'

'She looks like a Carnival Queen!' Fern said. She meant Judy, of course, who was all in white. A gleaming white top and pure white trousers, her long black hair tied back with a long white ribbon.

I started to feel a little uneasy. Fern had been right when she'd said Judy would go crazy if someone spilled anything on her. She'd hit the *roof*. Except that outside there wasn't a roof for her to hit. Which meant she'd probably go into *orbit*, and take me with her.

I guess this sounds kind of cowardly, but I was half hoping Amanda wouldn't show up. At least then I wouldn't get myself beaten to a pulp by Judy MacWilliams.

The three of them gathered around the barbecue to get some food.

'I've been thinking,' I said. 'Maybe Fern's idea about the phone call wasn't so crazy after all.' I looked at my three friends. 'Guys?' I said, hopefully. 'What do you say? I could tell her there was a phone call. Guys? Wouldn't that be better? Don't you think?'

'Are you getting cold feet?' Pippa asked.

'No,' I said. 'Not at all.' I gave them a weak grin. 'OK, I admit it. Yes. Judy will kill me.'

Fern reached across and patted me on the shoulder. 'A girl's gotta do what a girl's gotta do,' she said. 'Don't sweat it, Stacy. If she whacks you, we'll be right behind you.'

'I suppose you couldn't make that right in *front* of me? I asked.

'It was a democratically-arrived-at decision,' Pippa said. 'You can't back out now, Stacy.'

'I can't?'

'No.' Pippa said firmly. 'You can't.'

I watched as Greg, Karen and Judy filled their plates and sat on a rug over on one side near the patio.

I kept looking at my watch. Maybe Amanda wasn't coming after all? I lived in hope.

'Show time,' Fern said. I looked around.

There they were. The whole Bimbo brigade: Amanda, Cheryl Ruddick, Natalie Smith and Rachel Goldstein, chattering and laughing and making plenty of noise.

I saw Amanda look across at Greg and Judy. For a second she looked kind of annoyed, then she gave a big toss of her hair and said something to the others which made them all screech with laughter.

I waved at Amanda, but she ignored me. I

guess it wouldn't be grown-up enough for them to sit with us.

Then Greg called them over and they went and sat with them.

Cindy nudged me in the ribs. 'When are you going to do it?' she asked.

'Give me a chance,' I said. 'I can't just go over there and tip stuff on Judy. It's got to look like an accident.'

The way they were all chatting and laughing, you wouldn't have thought that Amanda and Judy hated each other. But those two are always like that. They're always real nice to each other face to face, even though it never fools anyone.

'I'm getting some more to eat,' Fern said. 'Anyone want a burger?'

I didn't feel like eating anything. Why do I let Pippa get me into these messes?

'Popcorn!' called Cindy's mother, carrying a big tub of the stuff out of the house.

'I'll go for that,' Pippa said, getting up.

Judy and a couple of the others got up as well. I figured this was my best chance. If there was a gang of us crowding around, I could have my 'accident' without it looking too obvious.

I went up there with the others and held out my plate to Mr Spiegel.

'Burger, steak or drumstick?' he asked.

I looked at the sizzling food. Now, which one would make the biggest mess?

'Steak, please,' I said.

'Hey, big appetite,' Mr Spiegel said with a smile. He forked up the dripping steak and slammed it down on my plate.

Judy was between me and the salad table, waiting while Mrs Spiegel scooped a paper carton into the popcorn for her. I saw Amanda standing right behind her.

Deep breath, Stacy. Don't think about it. Just do it.

I sidled toward Judy. I couldn't look. I pretended to stumble, and, with my eyes shut tight, I let my plate tip over and out of my hands.

'Hey! careful!' I heard Amanda yell.

I snapped my eyes open. As I'd tripped, Judy had done a sidestep and Amanda had moved forward. I'd bumped into the wrong person!

'Stacy!' Amanda yelled as the plate and the big juicy steak splatted onto her jeans. 'You idiot!'

I stared in disbelief. My plate was on the ground, face down, with the steak peeking out from under it. And there was a nice long greasy streak down the side of Amanda's jeans.

So Pippa wanted to know what could possibly go wrong? Now she knew.

8

I perched on the side of the bathtub in Cindy's bathroom. Amanda was at the sink, rubbing her jeans with a cloth.

'I'm going to enter you in the Dumb Olympics,' Amanda said, wetting the cloth and attacking the greasy stain again. 'Stacy Allen – the All-American Nerd champion!'

'It was an accident,' I said. 'I didn't know you were going to barge in like that.'

'You had your *eyes* closed.' Amanda said. She stopped rubbing and glared at me. 'What sort of dork walks around with her eyes closed?'

'I had the sun in my eyes,' I said. 'I only closed them for a second. How should I know you'd get in the way?' I sighed. 'All you had to do was keep back for a couple of seconds, and it could have worked perfectly. But could you do that? No, Amanda has to come shoving her way in.' I frowned at her. 'The way you *always* do!'

'Oh, I get it,' Amanda said. 'There was me thinking it was *your* fault, for walking around with your eyes shut. But all the time it was *my* fault for wanting some popcorn.' She rolled her eyes. 'Thanks for straightening me out, Stacy, you imbecile!'

'Well, that's the last time I try helping you out!' I said. 'I should have known better!'

Amanda stopped rubbing. 'Helping me out?' she said. 'What are you talking about?'

'I guess I might as well tell you,' I said. 'The steak was supposed to go down Judy's clothes, not yours.'

Amanda blinked at me. 'Huh?'

'It was all planned,' I said. 'Step 2. We had this *plan*, you see. The whole idea was to get Judy out of the way so you could get together with Greg.'

Amanda stared at me for a few moments. 'So I could *what*?'

'Look,' I said. 'I know you were really mad when Greg showed up with Judy the other night. I just wanted to help you out. I was supposed to spill stuff on Judy, then she'd have to go to the bathroom to clean up, and *you* could have had Greg to yourself for a while.' Amanda was still staring blankly at me. 'Don't you get it?' I asked.

'Are you crazy?' Amanda said.

'I guess I must be,' I said. 'Crazy for trying to help you out.'

'Do you mean you set up this whole deal – getting me to come to the barbecue and everything, just for *that*?' Amanda said. 'Do you know what Judy would have done to you if you'd got her with that steak? You'd have gone home in an ambulance!'

'Yeah, I know,' I said. 'And you had to go and mess it all up.'

'It's me who got messed up, you idiot,' Amanda said. 'Just look at these jeans! And do you really think I'd still want to go out with Greg Masterson after what happened on Friday night?'

'Huh?' I said in amazement. 'But you *like* him! You told me he was only with Judy because he was too scared to ask you out.'

'OK!' Amanda said angrily. 'So I was wrong! I was wrong about him! If you really want to know, I think Greg Masterson is the *dumbest* person in the whole country! No, the *second* dumbest. Judy MacWilliams is the dumbest. They *deserve* each other.'

'You mean he doesn't want to date you?' I asked. 'But you told me – '

'Never mind what I told you!' Amanda snapped. 'Judging by the way they were behaving on Friday night, I'd say he's *perfectly* happy with that jackass Judy. Have you got the picture now, Stacy? Have I made it *clear* enough for you?'

'But you were talking to him out there just now,' I said. 'I saw you.'

'Of course I was talking to him,' Amanda said. 'Do you think I'd give *either* of them the satisfaction of thinking I cared?'

'You mean, you don't?' I asked.

'No. I couldn't care less!' Amanda shouted. 'It's his loss, not mine!'

'So why are you yelling at me?'

'I'm yelling at you because my jeans are covered in grease,' Amanda shouted. 'I'm yelling at you because you're the dumbest kid sister a person ever had to put up with!'

'So I went to all this trouble to try and get you a date with a guy you don't even *like* any more?' I yelled. I figured it was my turn to get mad. Why couldn't Amanda have just told me all this before? 'Why didn't you say something?'

'Like what?' Amanda said. 'Like, "Don't fix me up with Greg Masterson"? How was I supposed to know you were going to pull a dumb stunt like that?'

There was a knock on the bathroom door.

'Is everything OK in there?' It was Luke's voice.

'Yes, thanks,' Amanda called. 'Everything's just fine.'

'Did you get the stain out?' Luke called.

Amanda took a look at her jeans. They were wet all down one side, but you could still see the greasy patch. 'Not really,' Amanda called to him.

'Would you like to borrow a pair of my jeans?' he called through the door. 'They'll be too big for you, but you could hold them up with a belt.'

Amanda went over and unlocked the door.

'Thanks, Luke,' she said. 'That would be really nice of you.'

Wow! Talk about a fast mood change! One second she's behaving like she wants to stuff me down the sink. The next second she's being all sweetness and light with Luke.

'It's nothing,' Luke said with a grin. 'You can't go around all afternoon smelling like steak. Every dog in the neighbourhood would be following you around.' He had a pair of jeans over his arm.

Amanda took them from him and closed the door again.

'Now, that,' she said to me as she changed, 'is what I call being *helpful*, Stacy. Get the picture?'

I sure did. Amanda just didn't appreciate what I'd been trying to do for her!

★ ★ ★

I went back out into the yard. Pippa, Fern and Cindy gave me anxious looks as I went and sat on the blanket with them.

Fern looked all over me.

'What?' I said.

'I'm just checking for bruising,' she said. 'The way Amanda looked, I thought she was going to tie you in *knots* up there. What happened?'

I told them about it.

'It looks like you really messed up this time, Stacy,' Pippa said.

'Me?' I said. 'It was *your* plan!'

'Yeah, but I was only working on what you told me,' Pippa said. 'You didn't take the X factor into account.' She shook her head. 'You've always got to watch out for the X factor, Stacy.'

'What's that?' Cindy asked.

'The human element,' Pippa said. 'Whenever you come up with a plan, you should always take the human element into account. That's the X factor.'

'I guess my sister is more X than most people,' I said.

'You can say that again,' Fern said with a grin.

A little while later Amanda came out wearing Luke's jeans. They were really baggy, and she had to turn the legs up, but she was smiling and talking to Luke, so I guess she wasn't too mad about the whole thing. Just mad at *me*!

I looked over at Greg, sitting on the rug with Judy and the rest of the Bimbos. One minute Amanda is crazy to go out with him, and the next she says she wouldn't touch him with a ten-foot pole. I mean, how's a person supposed to figure these things out?

Teenagers sure are weird.

'Coming to get some more to eat?' Fern asked me.

'No way,' I said. 'The way my luck's been going this afternoon, I really *will* spill it all on Judy!'

The rest of the afternoon was a lot less eventful. The only other piece of excitement was when Denny fell into a rose-bush during a game of tag and had to go get himself bandaged up.

The cookout began to break up. Amanda and the Bimbos went off somewhere and the grown-ups went indoors. Pippa and Fern headed off a little while later, and I stayed to help clean up with Cindy and Luke.

Actually, Luke did most of the work. Cindy and I finished off the popcorn before we joined in.

'Did you and your friends have a good time?' he asked, as I helped him to fill a black garbage sack with leftover scraps and empty cans. He grinned. 'Was your sister mad at you about the accident?'

'No more than usual,' I said. 'She's kind of difficult at times, but I've gotten used to it.'

'Artistic temperament, huh?' Luke said. 'She told me she does a lot of painting and stuff. It sounds interesting. We talked a while.' He smiled at me. 'I really enjoyed talking to her.'

I didn't know what to say to that. I guess Amanda can be charming when she wants to be. She sure seemed to have turned on the charm for Luke.

★ ★ ★

I was in for a surprise when I got home.

'Stacy!' Dad called from the living room. 'In here a minute.'

He was stretched out on the carpet with Sam. There were coloured building blocks all over. Dad was trying to build Sam a house, but Sam seemed more interested in throwing the blocks around the room.

Dad grinned at me. 'I guess he isn't going to be an architect when he grows up,' he said. Sam picked up a red block and sucked on it.

I sat down with them.

'You had a visitor,' Dad said, sitting up. 'Ouch!' He lifted himself and pulled a block out from under him. He handed it to Sam. A green one. Sam sucked it.

'Do green ones taste different, Sam?' I asked.

Sam made a face and threw the block away.

Dad laughed. 'I guess that one wasn't ripe yet,' he said.

'Who was it?' I asked.

'Huh?'

'My visitor?'

'Davey from across the street,' Dad said. 'He left you a present.' He pointed at the coffee-table. On it was a plate, and sitting on the plate were six chocolate cookies.

'I think you have an admirer,' Dad said.

I stared at the cookies. 'What did he say?'

'Not much,' Dad said. 'The doorbell rang and he was just standing there with the plate. He said, "I promised Stacy she could have some cookies." ' Dad grinned at me. 'That was about it.'

'He's weird,' I said.

'Hey,' Dad said, 'he's just shy. I think he likes you.'

'Well, he can quit liking me right now,' I said. 'I don't want him coming over here with cookies all the time. Is he nuts, or what?'

Dad smiled. 'You can ask him when you take the plate back,' he said.

'No way am I doing that,' I said. 'I never asked for any cookies. If he wants his plate back, he can come and get it himself.' I got up. 'And I'm not answering the door to him, either.'

I ran up to my room and shut myself in. The last thing in the *world* I needed was Davey Brown coming over here and leaving me presents.

I decided to spend some time working on my butterfly poster. I'd already coloured most of the butterflies by then, but there were a lot of curly leaves and vines still left to do. I got out the poster and spread it on the floor. That was when I remembered that Amanda had taken back the magic markers I'd been using.

It isn't usually a great idea just to take stuff from Amanda's room without asking. She doesn't like me even going *in* there without filling out a form in triplicate first. But she wasn't at home to ask, so I decided to risk it.

Amanda's room is such a mess. If she kept everything in some kind of *order*, I'd have been able to find the markers and get out of there without searching.

And if I hadn't been searching, I guess I wouldn't have spotted her diary lying open on her desk.

Now, I'm not the kind of person who usually pokes their nose into another person's diary. It just happened to be open and I couldn't help seeing the entry she'd made on Friday night.

I mean, it was written in red ink. In big letters. I couldn't *help* reading it.

It said: *GREG AND JUDY MAKE ME SICK. I WISH SOMEONE WOULD INTRODUCE ME TO SOME INTERESTING BOYS!*

Someone? Hmmm . . . maybe there was a way for me to make up to Amanda for the problems she'd had with Greg.

Yeah, why not? Amanda would be really pleased if I helped her find an interesting boyfriend. And it would be a good way of proving to her that I wasn't as dumb as she thought.

Watch out, world: here comes Stacy the Matchmaker!

One of the places I like to hang out with my friends is Maynard Park. It's right in the middle of town, but you wouldn't know it, because of all the trees and bushes. When you're in the middle of the park you can't see any buildings at all.

There's a playground for little kids. When Sam's a little older I'll be able to bring him along there for rides on the swings and slides. There's a fountain right in the middle of the park. It looks kind of like a big candlestick with water coming out of the top.

But our favourite place is over by the ponds. Maynard Park has got three ponds, linked by these shallow streams of crystal-clear water. There's a stone bridge over one of the streams, and when you hang over the side of the bridge, you can see down to the bottom of the stream.

The four of us were playing Duck Derby on Monday afternoon after school. There are a whole bunch of ducks that live on the ponds.

Duck Derby is where we hang over the upstream side of the bridge and wait for some ducks to come swimming along. Then we each pick a duck and go running over to the other side of the bridge to see whose duck appears first. To make it more interesting we give the ducks names.

'Yo! Surf King, the Wonder Duck!' Fern yelled as we leaned over the bridge and saw the first duck come scooting out. 'Champion duck!'

'That's not Surf King,' Cindy said. 'That's Thunderball.'

The problem with Duck Derby is that, apart from the fact that the girl ducks are brown and the boy ducks are greeny-blue, they all look pretty much the same.

I guess *they* can tell each other apart, but from where we were, the first duck out from under the bridge could have been Surf King, the Wonder Duck *or* Thunderball.

I wasn't really in the mood for Duck Derby that afternoon. I was still thinking about the entry in Amanda's diary. I hadn't told my friends about it yet. Things you may happen to see in people's private diaries must *always* be kept secret, but I trusted my friends not to spread it around. And besides, if I was going to do some matchmaking on Amanda's behalf, I'd need their help.

I told them about Amanda's diary entry for Friday.

'She wishes someone would introduce her to some interesting boys?' Fern said. 'Is she kidding? There's no such thing.'

'*We* don't have to think they're interesting,' Pippa said. 'It's *Amanda* who has to think they are.' She looked at me. 'What's Amanda's idea of interesting?'

Good question. I thought about it. What exactly *did* Amanda mean by interesting?

'I know what I'd find interesting,' Cindy said. 'A boy who worked in Disneyland.'

'You want to date Goofy?' Fern said.

'That's not what I meant,' Cindy said. 'I was thinking more of a boy who worked there and said, "Hey, how about you and some friends coming down here for a free trip?"'

'Golddigger!' Pippa said.

'I am not,' Cindy said. 'Anyway, what's a golddigger?'

'A girl who gets guys to take her on free trips to Disneyland,' Pippa said.

Cindy shook her head. 'I wouldn't want him to *take* me,' she said. 'Just *pay* for me.'

'An astronaut!' Fern said. 'Astronauts are interesting.'

'Cool,' I said. 'If Amanda had an astronaut boyfriend, maybe he'd take her off to the moon.' I thought about it. Was the moon far enough? 'Or perhaps Mars?'

'I'd want a boyfriend who lived in California,' Fern said. 'One who lived in a big house on the beach. Like in the movies.' She hitched herself up on to the parapet of the bridge and stretched out. 'And I'd lie in the sun all day eating candy and drinking strawberry shakes.'

'My boyfriend would have to be a forest ranger, or something like that,' I said. 'And he'd have to be able to pilot a helicopter, so he could take me to see the Grand Canyon and Yosemite Park. Or he could be one of those guys who save rhinos.'

'Rhinos?' Pippa said. 'In Yosemite Park?'

'In *Africa*,' I said. 'Like in the nature programmes on TV... But we're not talking about *us*. We're talking about Amanda. What kind of guy would *she* like?'

'You tell us,' Pippa said. 'You know her better than we do.'

'Which rock stars does she like?' Cindy asked.

'Oh, the usual ones,' I said. 'But that doesn't help. We're not going to get her a date with a rock star.'

'Hold it,' Fern said. 'How come we're suddenly talking about fixing Amanda up a date again? We tried that already.'

'Yeah,' I said. 'But that was with the wrong boy. That's why we've got to really think about it this time, so we come up with the *right* boy.'

'Like who?' Pippa asked.

'I don't know,' I said. 'If I'd thought of someone already I wouldn't be asking you guys about it.'

'If you want my opinion,' Fern said, 'you're just asking for trouble.'

'Not if we find the perfect boy,' I said. 'I'm sure we could come up with some interesting boys for her to meet if we really tried.'

'Why us?' Pippa asked.

'Because Amanda is mad at me,' I explained. 'She thinks I'm just a dumb kid. I want to prove her wrong.'

'But she thinks that because you tried to fix her up with Greg,' Cindy said. 'So how does doing the same thing all over again make things better?'

'It won't *be* the same thing all over again,' I said. 'The idea was fine, but Greg was the wrong boy. We need to come up with someone else. Someone Amanda would *really* like to go out with.'

'Yeah, and preferably someone who's not going out with Judy MacWilliams,' Fern said.

'But how do we do that?' Cindy asked. 'We don't even know what kind of boys Amanda would find interesting.'

'We could find out,' Pippa said.

'How do we do that?' Cindy asked.

'Easy.' Pippa held up one finger. 'First,' she said, 'we need to get a list of things that Amanda finds interesting.'

'I can tell you that,' I said. 'Blabbing to her Bimbo friends, cheerleading and looking at herself in a mirror.'

'I meant about *boys*,' Pippa said. 'Anyone got a pen and paper? We could make a list of questions to ask her.'

'You mean like a dating agency?' Cindy said.

Pippa nodded. 'And then, when we've got that,' she lifted a second finger, 'we look around at school for any guys who fit Amanda's list.'

'And then?' I asked.

'We arrange for them to meet,' Pippa said.

'Amanda's not going to meet up with some guy just because we say so,' I pointed out. 'That's the last thing she'd do.'

'So we do it without her realizing,' Pippa said. 'We do it sneakily.'

'It sounds like it might be a lot of fun,' Fern said. 'Come on, you guys, who's got some paper? Let's get some questions written down.'

I found some paper in my bag and we sat in a circle on the grass at the end of the bridge.

'OK,' Pippa said. 'Hit me with some questions.'

' "Would your perfect boyfriend have blue or brown eyes?" ' Cindy said. 'Put that down for a start.'

Pippa started scribbling.

' "Would it be OK if he had crossed eyes?" ' Fern said, crossing her own.

' "Dark hair or blond hair?" ' I said.

' "Or no hair at all",' Fern giggled.

'Fern!' Pippa said. 'You're not helping.'

'Some girls go for bald guys,' Fern said. 'My dad's almost bald, and my mom doesn't seem to mind.'

'But was your dad bald when your mom met him?' Cindy asked.

'Um . . . I guess not,' Fern said. 'OK. Leave out the question about bald guys. But you could include a question about cars. Like, "What car would your perfect boyfriend drive?" '

'What sort of boys do you think we're trying to fix Amanda up with?' I asked. 'She's thirteen. She's not going to date boys who can drive.'

'So ask her what kind of car they'd *like* to drive,' Fern said. 'Oh, and you'd better put something in about how much money they're prepared to spend. You don't want Amanda ending up with some dead-beat who has to borrow money off her to get home.'

'Don't you think we ought to ask questions about music and sports, and stuff like that?' Cindy said.

'Good idea, at *last*,' Pippa said, frowning at Fern. 'I'm glad someone's brain is working. OK, "What kind of music and sports would your perfect boyfriend have to like?" Um, what else is Amanda interested in, Stacy?'

'Art,' I said. 'And clothes. Oh, and movies. Mention movies.'

'OK,' Pippa said. 'I'll include a question about that. And you'd better ask her what kind of place she'd like to go on a first date.'

Pippa scribbled some more and then handed me the sheet of paper.

'There you go,' she said. 'Try these on her.'

'I don't know,' I said. 'I don't want her to know what we're planning. She'll know I'm up to something if I shove a list of questions about boys in her face.' I said. 'Even Amanda's not that dumb.'

'You don't do it like that,' Pippa said. 'You ask her *casually*, so she doesn't suspect anything.'

'OK,' I said dubiously. 'I'll give it a try.'

Casually? Now, how was I going to get a whole bunch of answers out of Amanda without her getting suspicious?

Well, I had one advantage. At least I had a brain in my head, unlike *some* sisters I could mention. And, the way that list had filled out, it looked like my brain was in for a busy time.

10

I started doing my homework as soon as I got home that afternoon. I could hear music coming from Amanda's room. Music through the wall is really distracting. But it's not half as distracting as having Benjamin come in and sit in the middle of the book I was trying to copy from.

'Don't you want me to learn about the Panama Canal?' I asked him.

'Mrrrp,' he said, stretching out on my textbook.

'I guess that means no,' I said.

To be honest, it wasn't just Benjamin that was distracting me. It was the list of questions I was supposed to ask Amanda. I still hadn't figured out how I was going to get the answers without making her suspicious.

I pushed Benjamin's tail out the way and started writing again.

'The Panama Canal', I wrote, 'was built between 1904 and 1914, to link the Atlantic and Pacific Oceans.' Benjamin's tail came back over the page.

'Wouldn't you like to go chase some birds?' I asked him. Benjamin is always chasing birds, but he's never caught any. They just fly up out of the way and sit there laughing at him. Not that he's put off by that. He just goes right on chasing them.

A paw came flicking out and jogged my pen.

'That's it,' I said. 'I give up.' The Panama Canal would have to wait; Benjamin wanted to play.

I tossed my eraser across the floor and Benjamin went diving after it. Benjamin likes beating up my eraser.

I was still playing chase-the-eraser with Benjamin when the doorbell rang. I heard Amanda go to answer it. A few seconds later, she hammered on my door.

'It's for you,' she shouted.

She was standing there with a big grin on her face.

'What's so funny?' I asked.

'Go see,' she said. She patted me on the head. (I hate that!) 'If you need any advice on how to handle boys, just ask,' she said.

It was Davey Brown. Talk about embarrassing. He was standing there with this big dopey smile on his face. Why me? Why was he picking on me?

'Did you like the cookies?' he asked.

'Yes, thanks,' I said. 'Wait there, I'll just get the plate.' I hadn't even touched his cookies. I slid them on to another plate and went back into the hall.

'Do you want to come and see my rabbits?' he asked. 'I've got two. They're called George and Martha.'

'Gee, sorry,' I said. 'I'm real busy right now. Maybe some other time?'

I shut the door quickly. What was going on? First he started talking to me in the street, then he brought cookies over and now he wanted me to go see his rabbits.

'You didn't tell me you had a boyfriend.' Amanda was sitting at the top of the stairs.

'I don't!'

'If you say so,' Amanda said with a big grin.

'Will you quit that!' I said. I really wished Davey hadn't come over like that. It was so embarrassing. Or if he *had* to, he could at least have done it when Amanda wasn't around.

'Don't you like him?' Amanda asked. 'He seems OK.'

'You go look at his rabbits, if you're so interested,' I said.

'OK,' Amanda said, standing up. 'But like

I said – if you want any advice on boys, you know where to come.'

Benjamin had wandered off somewhere when I got back up to my room, which meant that I could finish my homework.

Then I had another of my brainwaves. Maybe Davey Brown wasn't such a pain after all.

I took a quick look at the list of questions I was supposed to ask Amanda, then went down the hall to her room.

She was lying on her bed reading a magazine.

'Hey, Amanda?' I said. 'Can I ask you something?'

'Fire away,' Amanda said.

'What would you look for in the perfect boyfriend?' I asked.

'What would *I* look for?' Amanda said with a laugh. 'Well, he'd have to come up with something a little better than cookies and pet rabbits.' She gave me a really smug look. 'But then the kind of guys I'd date would have to be a little more grown-up than Davey Brown.'

Can you believe how stuck-up she is? Anyone would think she'd been dating boys for *years*. I mean, she'd only been on *one* date, and that had been a total disaster.

I went for the big question. 'So what would you find interesting in a boy?'

'Well,' Amanda said, giving me her big voice-of-authority look. 'He'd need to be good-looking. I couldn't go around with some *freak*. And he'd need to be interested in the kind of things I'm interested in – otherwise we wouldn't have anything to talk about.'

'But you're not interested in *anything*,' I said. 'Apart from clothes and hairdos and cheerleading.'

'I am, too, interested in other things,' Amanda said. 'There's a whole bunch of things, for your information.'

'OK,' I said. 'Don't get mad. I was only *asking*.'

'Anyone would think I was a total airhead, the way you talk,' Amanda said.

'You said it.' Me and my big mouth! But Amanda really does sit up and *beg* for it, sometimes.

'I'm smarter than *you*,' Amanda said. 'At least I know how to have fun. You wouldn't know fun if it came up and bit you on the nose!'

'I have plenty of fun!' I said. 'At least I don't spend half my life looking in a mirror.'

Amanda laughed. 'I wouldn't either, if I had

a face like yours!' she said. 'Hasn't anyone told you freckles are *out* this year?'

'You just shut up about my freckles,' I yelled. 'Mom says freckles are cute.'

'Yeah,' Amanda said. 'About as cute as a brace, metal-mouth.' Metal-mouth! Grr!

'At least in a couple of years I'm going to have straight teeth,' I said. 'Your *brain* is going to be crooked for your whole life!'

'If I'm so dumb,' Amanda said. 'How come you're in here asking me for advice?'

Yeah, right! I came in here to get those questions answered. At this rate we'd barely end up speaking to each other.

'Oh, forget it,' I said. 'I'll go ask the cat. He's smarter than you, anyhow.'

As far as I was concerned right then, Amanda could find her *own* boyfriend. I'd had it with trying to help her out.

'Hey!' Amanda shouted as I walked out. 'You borrowed my magic markers again without asking! I want them back!'

Weather Report: storms, typhoons and hurricanes heading this way from the direction of Amanda's room. Lock all doors and keep under cover.

In other words: situation normal in the Allen household.

★ ★ ★

I met up with the other guys the following morning in school. I'd planned on telling them the whole boyfriend thing was off. But Pippa thought otherwise.

'Look,' she said, after I'd told them about the argument I'd had with Amanda. 'Weren't you saying that you wanted to get Amanda a boyfriend so she'd realize what a great sister you are?'

'I guess so,' I said.

'And does she think you're great right now?' Pippa asked.

'Not so you'd notice,' I said. 'But I don't feel like helping her out now.'

'The way I see it,' Cindy said reasonably, 'you'll be helping yourself out. If you find a boyfriend for her, think how grateful she'll have to be.'

'And it'll be fun,' Fern said.

I looked at her. Fun? Amanda had said I didn't know how to have fun. That tipped the scales.

'OK,' I said. 'But I'm not going to ask her any more questions. I'll only end up fighting with her. We'll just have to do some guesswork.'

Just then the buzzer sounded for first

period, so we decided we'd talk about it at lunch.

★ ★ ★

We sat at our favourite table in the cafeteria. The reason it's our favourite is because it's way over in a corner, which means you don't get people barging past you all the time. It's also a good place to have private conversations.

I got out a notebook and wrote down a few things that I knew Amanda would insist on: *Good-looking. Must like music. Must like going to the movies. Must like sports.*

'OK,' Cindy said. 'So who do we know around here who fits all those things?' Our first plan was to try and find someone who went to our school.

'Andy Melniker?' Fern suggested.

'Are you nuts?' I shrieked. 'Andy Melniker is in our grade. Amanda's not going to date a ten year-old!'

'Why not?' Fern said. 'My Dad is three years younger than my Mom, and they get along OK.'

'Fine,' I said. 'That's just fine, Fern. Maybe you could suggest a few kids from kindergarten, too? I'm sure Amanda would have a great

103

time, pushing her boyfriend around in a baby carriage.'

'How about Brad Schnieder?' Cindy said.

'That's more like it,' I said. I wrote his name down. Brad Schnieder was in Amanda's grade. He was a tall, skinny guy with his hair down over his eyes. 'But is he Amanda's type?' I said, sucking my pen to help me think.

'Well, he plays guitar,' Cindy said. 'And he's in the drama group. Don't you remember? He was in the end of year production of *Swiss Family Robinson.*'

'What about sports?' I said.

'I've seen him with ice-skates,' Pippa said.

'Good,' I said. 'That'll do for a start. And if he's into act ng, I guess he must like movies.'

'What about Tony Scarfoni?' Fern said. 'All the eighth-grade girls are crazy about him.' Tony Scarfoni is captain of the football team.

'He's going out with Shirley Waterstone,' Pippa said. 'I can't see Amanda coming out on top in a battle with *her.*' Shirley wasn't what you'd call cute; she was the Four Corners inter-school discus-throwing champion. Her arms were thicker than my waist! Anyone trying to muscle in on her boyfriend would have to like the taste of hospital food.

'Jake Emmett?' Cindy said. 'He's great at

gymnastics, and he swims. *And* he's in the basketball team.'

'And he's real intelligent,' Pippa said.

'Amanda didn't say anything about wanting an *intelligent* boyfriend,' I pointed out.

'Yeah, but think of the advantages,' Cindy said. 'He could help her with her homework.'

'OK,' I said. I wrote his name down. 'At least that would save *me* having to help her all the time. Anyone else?'

We spent the rest of break going through all the eighth-grade boys we could think of. But by the end we still only had the two names we'd come up with first: Brad Schnieder and Jake Emmett.

'Right,' I said. 'Let's get to work. *Operation Matchmaker.*' I grinned at them. 'By the end of the week, guys, we're going to have fixed it so Amanda has herself a boyfriend, or my name's not Stacy Allen!'

11

It's one thing picking out a couple of guys that Amanda might want to date. It's something *else* trying to come up with some realistic way of actually getting the thing off the ground.

We were still talking about it after school. And we still hadn't come up with any good ideas.

'We should approach this systematically,' Pippa said. 'Formulate a coherent plan of action and adopt a scientific approach.' I hope *she* knew what that meant, because I sure didn't. I guess having a college professor for a mom does weird things to your head. It certainly did weird things to Pippa's vocabulary.

'I think we should just work on one of them at a time,' I said. 'It's going to be too complicated otherwise.'

'OK,' Cindy said. 'Let's vote on the lucky guy.'

'You mean, the one who *isn't* going to date Amanda?' Fern joked.

'No,' Cindy said. 'The one who *is*. OK, hands up for Brad Schnieder.'

Fern and Pippa put their hands up.

'And for Jake Emmett?' Cindy said.

Cindy and I both put our hands up. Thinking it over, I decided that a guy who was good at sports and who was intelligent as well would be just right for Amanda. Sure, she hadn't included 'intelligent' in her list, but, come on, who wants to date a dummy?

'Tie,' Fern said. '*Now* what do we do?'

'Let's try this one more time,' I said. 'Bearing in mind that Amanda is *my* sister, and I vote for Jake. OK, who's for Brad Schnieder?'

Pippa and Fern put their hands up again. So much for my attempts at rigging the vote.

'Jake?' I said. Cindy voted with me again.

Fern grinned. 'Maybe Amanda should have a vote?' she said.

'I can see only one way out of this,' Pippa said. 'Why don't Fern and I work on Brad, and you and Cindy see how you do with Jake?'

'Hey,' Fern said, 'a race! First pair to fix them up wins!'

'That's fine by me,' I said.

'Wait a second,' Pippa said. 'If this is a race, we've got to have some ground rules. Like for instance, Stacy isn't allowed to talk to Amanda about it.'

'That's OK,' I said. 'We were going to do it without telling Amanda anyway. That's the whole point. It's going to be a nice surprise for her.'

That settled it. I looked at Cindy. 'How about our team go back to my house for a planning session?' I suggested.

'And may the best team win,' Pippa said.

We split up, and Cindy and I caught the bus home.

'Hi, Mom!' I called, as we walked through the door.

'Hi, Stacy,' Mom called from the kitchen. 'Oh, hi, Cindy, how are you?'

'Fine, thanks, Mrs Allen,' Cindy said.

'How would you two girls like to mow the lawn for me?' Mom asked. 'There's a carton of ice-cream in the freezer; you can have it as a reward.'

'Sure,' I said.

'Can I phone home and tell my mom I'll be late?' Cindy asked.

'Go right ahead,' Mom said. 'And you can tell her you'll be staying for dinner, if you'd like to.'

While Cindy was on the phone, I got the lawnmower out.

'Where's Amanda?' I asked.

'I think she's over at Cheryl's house,' Mom said.

'That figures,' I said. 'Anything to get out of doing any chores around here.'

'I'm popping next door for a word with Mrs Lloyd,' Mom said. 'Sam's asleep upstairs, so keep one ear out for him, OK?'

'Will do.'

Cindy and I took turns with the mower; it wasn't long before the grass catcher was full. We were just heading up the lawn to get a bag for the grass clippings, when Luke appeared around the side of the house.

'I rang the bell,' he said. 'But no one heard me.' We hadn't heard the doorbell above the noise of the mower.

'You're just the guy we need,' I said. 'Five minutes' mowing gets you a share of our ice-cream.'

'That sounds fair,' Luke said with a smile. I was really beginning to like Luke. It seemed a shame he wouldn't be around long.

'What are you doing here?' Cindy asked. 'Are you looking for me?'

'I came by to pick up my jeans,' he said. 'I loaned them to Amanda at the barbecue, remember. Is she home?'

'I'm afraid not,' I said. 'Wait here, though. I'll see if I can find them for you.'

I went up to Amanda's room to look for Luke's jeans. I should have known better. You could lose an entire clothes store in there. I don't know how Amanda ever finds *anything* in that mess.

I couldn't find Luke's jeans anywhere.

On the way through the kitchen I got the ice-cream out of the freezer. Luke had just finished with the mower and was helping Cindy dump the rest of the clippings into the bag.

'I can't find your jeans right now,' I told him.

'No problem,' Luke said. 'I can come by another time. I guess someone like Amanda has a pretty busy social life, huh?'

'She gets around,' I said. 'If I'm lucky, sometimes I don't get to run into her for days on end.'

Luke gave me a strange look. 'If you're lucky?' he said. 'Don't the two of you get along very well?'

'You could say that,' I said. 'But, she's OK, really.' Amanda might drive me crazy at times, but I don't like to bad-mouth her in front of other people. (Except for Cindy, Pippa and Fern, of course, but that's different. They're my best friends.)

'So she goes out a lot?' Luke asked as he

110

carried the bag of clippings up to the side of the house.

'Yeah,' I said, 'and when she's not *out*, she's on the phone *planning* to go out.' I grinned. 'You've got to get up pretty early to catch Amanda.'

Luke gave me another strange look. 'I guess I can get up early,' he said.

Now what the heck did he mean by that?

We sat out back and took turns scooping ice-cream out of the carton. After a while, Luke said he had to be going.

'Tell Amanda I came by,' he said. 'It's not urgent, but I'd kind of like my jeans back before we leave. Maybe she could give me a call?'

'I'll tell her,' I said.

Cindy and I sat with a couple of milkshakes, breathing in the scent of the new-mown grass, which is one of the nicest smells in the world. It always makes me think of long hot summer vacations.

'Luke seemed kind of interested in Amanda,' Cindy said.

'Yeah,' I said, 'it's a shame he's not going to be around much longer. We might have been able to fix something up there.'

'Speaking of which,' Cindy said, 'do you

have any idea how we're going to get Jake to ask Amanda out?'

'We could tell him she really likes him,' I said. 'We could tell him she's *dying* to go on a date with him, but is too shy to ask.'

'Do you think he'd go for that?' Cindy asked. 'He's more likely to think we're setting him up.'

'A note!' I said. 'We could put a note from Amanda in his locker.'

'Saying what?' Cindy asked.

'I'm thinking about it,' I said. 'Let's go inside. I need some cookies. I think better with cookies.'

Five minutes and three cookies later, I had a plan.

'Right,' I said, 'what do you think of this? We arrange it so that Amanda goes to the skating rink, say, Friday night. Then we put a note in Jake's locker on Friday afternoon. It could say something like: "I'll be at the skating rink tonight, if you want to come too. Signed, Amanda." We put it in his locker last thing in the afternoon, so he doesn't have any time to speak to Amanda about it.' I started on another cookie, to keep my brain working. 'Jake goes to the rink. He meets up with Amanda. They have a great time, and we win the bet with Pippa and Fern!'

'And what if he doesn't show?' Cindy asked.

'Then I guess we'll know he's not interested. But what do you say? Does it sound OK?'

'How do we know Amanda will be at the rink?' Cindy asked.

I grinned at her. 'Leave that to me.'

* * *

Dinner that evening was a giant take-out pizza that Mom had ordered. Amanda was home by the time it arrived, and we all sat around the kitchen table – Mom, Amanda, Cindy and me – helping ourselves to the big gooey, sticky wedges of pizza.

'Save some for Dad,' Mom said. 'I'll reheat it in the microwave for him.' Dad often gets home very late. It's a real treat when the whole family can sit down together for an evening meal.

'Yuck!' Amanda said, picking at her slice of pizza. 'Anchovies! I hate anchovies!'

'I'll swap them for these pieces of mushroom,' I said. If there's one thing I can't stand, it's mushrooms. I picked out the pieces and plonked them on Amanda's plate. Amanda flicked a few strips of anchovy on to my pizza.

'Remind me never to take you to a high-class restaurant,' Mom said. 'Anyone would think I never taught you any table manners.'

She looked at Cindy. 'Does your family behave this badly, Cindy?' she asked.

Cindy laughed. 'Worse,' she said. 'You wouldn't want to *know* what Denny and Bob are like at the table.'

'Mom,' I said. 'Is it OK if I go ice-skating on Friday?'

'Sure. Try to come back with fewer bruises this time.'

Certain parts of me were black and blue when I got home from my last visit to Paradice. That was because *someone* decided to teach me how to skate backward. ('I'll show you,' Pippa had said. 'It's *easy*!' Easy? I had to eat standing up for two days!)

I looked at Amanda. 'Would you like to come ice-skating with me on Friday?' I asked her.

'No way,' Amanda said through a mouthful of pizza.

'But I'd really like to learn how skate backward. You're so good at it,' I said. 'I thought maybe you could teach me how it's done.'

Amanda shook her head. 'I'm busy Friday,' she said.

'Doing what?' Mom asked her.

Amanda shrugged. 'I don't know yet.'

'So why don't you go skating with Stacy?' Mom asked. 'Come on, you'd enjoy it.'

I'd been hoping Mom would say that. I'd mentioned it in front of her deliberately.

'How about it, Amanda?' I asked. 'You could teach me how to do all that neat stuff you do. I'd really appreciate a few lessons from an expert.' I know how to soften Amanda up. Flattering Amanda is like giving cream to a cat. You could almost hear her purring.

Amanda looked at Mom. 'Do I have to?' she said.

'No,' Mom said 'you don't *have* to. But, I think it would be nice of you to take your sister out occasionally.'

'OK,' Amanda said reluctantly. 'I'll put everyone else off on Friday, and I'll take my little sister skating.' She looked at me. 'But I'm not spending the whole time giving you lessons, OK?'

I smiled. 'With a teacher like you, it won't take ten minutes,' I said. Talk about a snow job. This was more like an avalanche!

But it was all I wanted to hear. I didn't mind Amanda being reluctant. The important thing was to get her there.

Now all we had to do was make sure Jake turned up.

12

I went along for the ride when Mom drove Cindy home later that evening. We sat in the back seat, discussing our plan in lowered voices.

'That was real neat,' Cindy whispered. 'But what are you going to do on Friday when Jake arrives?'

'That's where you come in,' I whispered back. 'I want you to be there, too. Keep your eyes open, and when you see Jake arrive, I want you to accidentally bump into me. I'll fall over and pretend I've hurt my ankle. You help me off the ice. I'll tell Amanda I need a little rest.' I grinned. 'And then we can watch what happens from the side.'

I had it all mapped out. Amanda keeps on skating. Jake comes sliding up to her. Their eyes meet. Romantic music fills the air. They take each other's hands and go into this really brilliant skating routine. Gradually the other people on the ice move away in awe. The

116

entire ice-rink is clear. Amanda and Jake spin and jump and twirl as the music reaches a crescendo. They come to a dramatic stop in a spray of ice, and everyone bursts into spontaneous applause.

Romance on ice! And all thanks to Stacy.

'OK,' Cindy whispered, bringing me back from my daydream. 'I just hope this "accident" works a little better than the last one.'

'It will,' I said. 'The last one was Pippa's idea. This one is all mine. It can't fail.'

'Are you going to tell Fern and Pippa about it?' Cindy asked.

'No way,' I said. 'This is a race, right?'

'What are you two whispering about back there?' Mom asked.

'Oh, nothing much,' I said.

'Hmmm,' Mom said. A guy can't even *whisper* around my mom without her thinking you're cooking something up. I sometimes think that moms are given a special *suspiciousness* injection in the hospital when they have babies. About the same time that they get that sixth sense thing that tells them when you're drinking milk straight from the carton instead of pouring it into a glass.

And, the way my mom behaves, I think she must have been given a *double* dose of suspiciousness.

117

* * *

Cindy and I met up with Pippa and Fern at school the next day.

'Have you come up with any ideas yet?' Pippa asked.

'Have *you*?' I asked right back.

'Maybe,' Fern said.

'Such as what?' Cindy asked.

'That would be telling,' Pippa said with a sneaky smile. 'You tell us first.'

'No way,' I said.

Fern looked at Pippa and grinned. 'They haven't come up with anything yet, I bet,' she said.

'Oh, yes we have,' Cindy said. 'We've fixed it so – '

'Cindy!' I interrupted. 'Don't go *telling* them. We don't want them stealing our ideas.'

'Huh!' Fern said. 'As if we *need* to! We've come up with a whole bunch of ideas.'

'Yeah,' I said. 'And knowing you two, they'll either be crazy or impossible.'

'Oh yeah?' Pippa said. 'We'll see about that!'

We still went around as a foursome that week, but every now and then I'd spot Fern and Pippa whispering together. The whispering would stop as soon as they saw me. *They* were making plans, too.

After school on Thursday, I found out *one* of the things they were whispering about.

When I got home I found Amanda in the kitchen, taking a pair of jeans out of the drier. 'Mom,' she called. 'Can you iron these for me?'

Mom was out in the yard with Sam. Mom had the wading pool out and Sam was sitting in the water, kicking and splashing and gurgling away happily. He was in the shade of the red-and-white striped parasol. Strong sunlight isn't good for baby skin, so Sam was sitting there all pink and naked under the parasol while Mom played with him.

'Put them with the rest of the stuff,' Mom called back. 'I'll do the ironing later.'

'But I need them done now,' Amanda said, giving the jeans a shake. 'I promised Luke I'd take them over to him this evening.' I'd passed on Luke's message to Amanda about the jeans. I guessed that she wanted them ironed right then because she'd called him and arranged to take them over to Cindy's house.

'So, do them yourself,' Mom called.

'Aw! *Mom!*' You should have seen Amanda's face! The Great Amanda Allen – *ironing*? To Amanda, that was the ultimate indication of nerdiness.

'What's with you?' Amanda asked me, as I grinned at her.

'Nothing,' I said. 'Shall I get you the iron?'

Amanda gave me a hopeful look. 'I don't suppose *you'd* do it for me?' she asked. 'You don't mind doing nerdy stuff like that.'

'Yeah,' I said. 'I'll do it. If you hold your breath while you're waiting.'

She stuck her tongue out at me.

'I'll iron *that* for you, though.' I said.

She went over to the back door.

'Mom? Please?' she said. 'It'll only take five minutes. I'll set the board up and everything.'

'OK.' Mom sighed. 'You come and keep an eye on Sam.'

* * *

Mom made one of her special tuna salads and we ate out in the yard while Sam crawled all over us. Sam's getting really good at crawling. You wouldn't believe how fast he can move. Twice I had to go and rescue him before he did a nosedive into the flower-beds. When he starts walking we're going to have to keep him on a leash, or he'll be at the other end of town before we can catch him.

A little later, Amanda put Luke's jeans in a bag and went off to Cindy's house. I was going to go along with her, but Mom said I should do my homework first.

The phone rang just as I was finishing. I thought it might be Cindy, so I went to answer it. 'Hello?' I said.

'Oh, hi. Uh, is Amanda there, please?' It was a boy's voice; he sounded a little nervous.

'Not right now,' I said. 'Would you like to leave a message?'

'Uh, yeah, could you tell her Brad called?'

Brad? My brain did a quick back-flip. Brad Schnieder! This just had to be something that Pippa and Fern had set up.

'Sure,' I said. 'I'll give her a note. Is there any other message you'd like me to give her?' I had to think quickly. No way was I going to let Brad talk to Amanda before Friday night if I could help it.

'Uh, no, I don't think so,' Brad said. I scribbled down his phone number and hung up.

Phew! I'd been lucky there. If Amanda had been in, that might have been the end of our race to fix her up with a date.

I thought through the rules we'd decided on. I'd promised not to take advantage of the fact that Amanda was my sister by talking to her about Jake. But was it cheating to take messages from Brad and then *hide* them?

I felt a little guilty as I pinned the note on

the board and covered it with Mom's list of babysitters. But like Fern had said at the barbecue, sometime a girl's just gotta do what a girl's gotta do. And I could always tell Amanda about the call *after* Friday evening.

I phoned Cindy to tell her what had happened.

'Did he say what he wanted?'

'Come *on*!' I said. 'You *know* what he wanted. Pippa and Fern must have said something to him.'

'Are you going to tell Amanda?' Cindy asked.

'Are you kidding?' I said. 'Not before Friday evening, that's for sure. And we've got to make sure Amanda doesn't get to speak to Brad tomorrow.'

'How are we going to do that?'

'I don't know just yet,' I said. 'But I'll think of something.'

Cindy laughed. 'We're sure keeping one step ahead of Fern and Pippa.'

'Yeah,' I said. 'Let's keep it that way. Have you talked to your folks about going to the rink tomorrow evening?'

'Uh, yeah . . .' Cindy's voice trailed off.

'Is there a problem?' I asked.

'I've got to bring Denny and Bob with me,' Cindy said.

Denny and Bob, the terrible twins.

I was just wondering how much of a problem Cindy's little brothers could turn out to be when the doorbell rang.

'There's someone at the door,' I told Cindy. 'Just a second.' I put my hand over the mouthpiece. 'I'll get it!' I yelled, to save Mom coming out.

I put the receiver down and answered the door.

Heck! Heck, heck and triple heck! Little Davey Brown *again*. 'Hi, Stacy,' Davey said.

'Hi, Davey,' I said. 'Sorry, I'm on the phone right now.' I crossed my fingers behind my back. 'One of my friends has got the flu. I've got to go see how she is as soon as I put the phone down.' Sometimes a white lie is the only way out. And I hoped it would stop him asking if I want to go see his darned rabbits.

'Oh, gee, that's too bad,' Davey said. 'I just came by to say I'm having a party on Saturday.' He looked at me with those big eyes of his. 'I wondered if you'd like to come?'

'Saturday?' I said. 'Oh, sorry, Davey. I'm going to be real busy on Saturday.' I didn't like being mean to the kid, but the last thing in the world I wanted to do was go to a party at Davey Brown's house. For starters, I knew for a *fact* that he didn't have any friends. For all I knew, I could be the only one he'd asked. I could see it now. Mr and Mrs Brown, Davey, me and the rabbits. No way!

He gave me a sad look. 'OK,' he said. 'I just thought I'd ask. Only, we're – '

'I can't really talk right now,' I interrupted him. The way he just stood there looking at me made me feel a little sorry for him. 'I hope you have a nice time, though,' I said. 'Sorry I can't make it.'

'That's OK,' he said.

I smiled so he wouldn't feel too bad. I mean, I don't *like* being unkind to people. But it was embarrassing! I just wished Davey would find some friends his own age and leave me alone.

He walked off, and I shut the door with a sigh of relief. I finished talking with Cindy and went into the living room.

'Who was that at the door?' Mom asked.

'Davey Brown again,' I said. 'He invited me to a party.'

'Davey? That's nice of him,' Mom said.

'No, it isn't,' I said. 'I told him I was busy.'

Mom frowned at me. 'Stacy! That wasn't very kind.'

'I know,' I said. 'But can I help it if he gives me the creeps?'

'He's only trying to be friendly,' Mom said. 'You could at least be nice to him.'

I shook my head. 'I can't,' I said. 'Come on, Mom. He's nine years old. He hasn't got any friends at all. He's weird. If I make friends with him, people will start thinking I'm weird, too.'

'I'm surprised at you, Stacy,' Mom said. 'I really didn't think you were like that.'

That made me feel even worse about myself. I could see that this whole business with Davey Brown was going to be a major headache.

Boys can really cause problems – even when you don't want to have anything to do with them.

13

I had a lot think about that evening. Now that I'd decided not to tell Amanda about Brad's call, I had to think up some way of keeping her away from him at school the next day.

And then it hit me. The perfect plan. If this worked, Amanda wouldn't let Brad get within ten yards of her.

Professor Von Allen of the Fly Right School of Behaviour: Stacy, are you sure this doesn't count as cheating?
Hey, I know. But come on – I put a lot of work into my plan with Jake. All I need is twenty-four hours. Is that so bad?

Gee, having a conscience can make things so difficult at times!

★   ★   ★

While Amanda and I were waiting for the school bus the next morning, I hit her with my Brad Schnieder avoidance plan.

126

'Did you know Brad Schnieder is looking for volunteers to help out with some play the drama group is setting up?' I asked her.

'No,' Amanda said. 'What play?'

'I don't know,' I said. 'All I heard was that he's looking for someone to paint some scenery. I'm surprised he hasn't asked you already. You did such a good job last term.'

I watched for Amanda's response. I wasn't disappointed; she gave me a look of pure horror.

'No *way* am I getting involved in anything like that again,' she said. 'They had me working like crazy last time.'

At the end of last term, Ms Guber, who runs the drama group, had talked Amanda into painting almost all the scenery for their play. (It was a musical version of *Swiss Family Robinson* – you know, the family that gets shipwrecked on a desert island and has to fight off pirates and wild animals.)

I can still remember Amanda arriving home late every day for a week, covered in blue paint. The entire backdrop for the play had been blue sky and blue sea. It had been two months before Amanda could even look at the colour without freaking out.

'Maybe you'd better steer clear of him if you don't want to do it again,' I told Amanda. I heard someone say yesterday he was planning on asking you.'

'Thanks for the warning. I'm going to keep right out of his way.'

I smiled to myself. From the determined look on Amanda's face, there was no way Brad Schnieder was going to get within two blocks of her today.

I met up with Cindy at school and told her what I'd done.

'But what happens when Amanda finds out there isn't any play?' she asked. I wish Cindy wouldn't keep coming up with these awkward questions.

'No sweat,' I told her. 'All she has to do is avoid Brad for one day. Once we've got Amanda and Jake together at the ice-skating rink, it won't matter.'

It was during lunch that I first saw for certain that my plan to keep Amanda and Brad apart was working. Cindy and I had gotten to our usual table before Fern and Pippa. Amanda was in the lunch line with some of her Bimbo pals.

I saw Brad Schnieder come into the cafeteria and start looking around. I nudged Cindy. Amanda took one look at Brad and did the quickest disappearing act you've ever seen in your life.

She dived under the counter and crept along on her hands and knees. At the far end, she took one quick look around and then zipped out through the exit like a gopher going into its hole. The other guys in line must have thought she'd flipped out.

'There goes one girl who doesn't want to paint any scenery!' I said to Cindy with a laugh.

'You've really got her on the run,' Cindy said. 'No way are Pippa and Fern going to win the race now.'

Cindy and I were on our way out when we bumped into Fern.

'Are you having any luck with Brad?' I asked her.

'I can't tell you,' Fern said with a big smile. 'It's a secret.' She looked at us. 'Unless you two feel like telling me how things are going with Jake.'

'We're doing OK,' I said. 'Where's Pippa?'

'That would be telling,' Fern said.

'Fine,' I said. 'But you can tell her from us that your guy doesn't stand a chance. We've got the whole thing sewn up.'

'You've fixed a *date*?' Fern said. 'A date for Jake?'

'Just about,' I said. 'I'll tell you all about it tomorrow.'

Fern stared at us as we walked away.

But one thing was bothering me. Where *was* Pippa? We decided it would be a good idea to go find her. In this kind of race, it's important to always know what your rivals are doing.

It took Cindy and me about ten minutes to track Pippa down. We finally found her out by the tennis courts. And she wasn't on her own. She was talking to Amanda.

'That's cheating!' I said. 'I bet she's trying to fix something up over there.'

'You don't know that,' Cindy said. 'They might be just chatting.'

'Huh!' I said. 'Since when did *any* of us have chats with Amanda? Pippa Kane is one big cheat!'

I was really annoyed. OK, so I'd done a couple of sneaky things to try and win the race, but at least I'd kept to the rule about not talking to Amanda.

We kept out of sight around the corner of the school building. It wasn't long before Pippa came walking in our direction with this huge smile on her face.

I stepped out of cover. '*We* saw you!' I said.

Pippa looked pretty startled. 'Oh. Hi, guys,' she said. 'Have you seen Fern?'

'Forget Fern,' I said. 'What were you talking to my sister about?'

'Nothing very much,' Pippa said, looking real shifty.

'What about the *rules*!' I said. 'None of us was supposed to talk to Amanda.'

'The rule was,' Pippa said, 'that we weren't supposed to talk to Amanda about Brad or Jake, and I wasn't.' She looked from me to Cindy. 'Honestly,' she said. 'I *wasn't*. I didn't mention Brad *once*. And that's the truth.'

'So what were you talking about?' Cindy asked.

Pippa shrugged. 'Nothing, really,' she said.

'Hmmm!' I said. It wasn't quite as good as one of my mom's 'hmmms', but then Mom's had a lot more practice than me.

'Don't you believe me?' Pippa said.

'I guess we do,' I said. After all, I was hardly in a position to get too high-and-mighty about cheating. Not after the way I'd warned Amanda to keep away from Brad.

'I should hope so,' Pippa said as she walked off. 'I'm going to find Fern. At least *she* knows I'm not cheating.'

'I think we upset her,' Cindy said. 'Hey, Stacy, let's go and make up. We don't want to make a big thing out of this.'

'We'll make up with her tomorrow,' I said. 'Anyway, it's her own fault if she won't tell us what she was talking to Amanda about.'

During the rest of lunch, Cindy and I worked on the note we were going to leave for Jake. (Remember? To put in his locker to make sure he came to the skating rink.) I'd already followed Jake earlier in the week to find out which locker was his.

'What about: "My darling Jake, I'm crazy with love for you"?' Cindy suggested with a grin. ' "My heart skips a beat every time you walk past me. I can't eat or sleep because I'm always thinking about you. When I look at the blackboard, all I see is your face. When the teacher speaks, all I hear is your voice. My love for you is making me ill. Only you can cure the ache that is in my heart"?'

We both fell around laughing as we thought how Jake would react to a note like *that*. The guy would just die of shock!

'How about: "I can't bear the thought of us being apart for another moment"?' I said. ' "Meet me in Paradice this evening and I will be yours for all eternity! We will make it a paradise for two. Yours until the stars fall from the sky. Amanda Allen." And then *twenty* Xs in a big heart-shape.'

In the end we decided to keep it simple: *I'm going to the skating rink this evening. Maybe we could meet up. It would be real nice if you could come along.*

We thought for a while about Xs, but decided not to put any. I did a fair imitation of Amanda's scrawly signature at the bottom of the note.

In a spare couple of minutes during the afternoon, I managed to sneak off to the hallway where Jake had his locker. I made sure there was no one around, and then made a dash for his locker. I'd planned on the whole operation taking about two seconds.

Aarrgh! I pushed and shoved at the note, but it wouldn't slide in under the door. Panic! What now? I smoothed out the crumpled note and tried again, looking up and down the hallway in case someone caught me.

Scrunch! The note was looking kind of battered now as I fought to get it in through the little gap.

Calm down, Stacy, I told myself. *It's too thick.* We'd folded the note into four. I opened it out and eased the corner in. Yes! I wiggled it, and it gradually slid in through the slit. It was almost in when it hit against something inside.

I looked at the half-inch of paper that still stuck out.

Then I heard voices. I whipped around with my back to the locker. A couple of teachers came around the corner. Mr Henderson and Mr Muller.

'Shouldn't you be in class?' Mr Henderson asked.

'I'm just going,' I said. I had one hand behind my back, desperately trying to cram that last half-inch of the note into Jake's locker.

'So go,' Mr Henderson said. He looked at me as I wriggled up against the locker. 'Are you OK?' he asked.

'Just fine,' I said, 'I just have this *itch*.' I felt the note slide the rest of the way in. I did some pretty impressive back-scratching as Mr Henderson and Mr Muller watched me walk down the hallway.

Phew! That was close! I hid around the corner until they were gone and then looked along the row of lockers. Great! You couldn't see the note at all. Mission accomplished!

* * *

'Are you ready yet?' Amanda hollered up the stairs.

I was in my room, burrowing under the bed to get my shoes.

'Just a minute!' I yelled. Benjamin thought it was a game. As I tried to yank my shoe out, he launched a claw into the trailing lace.

'Benjamin!' I said. 'Cut it out. I'm not playing!' I got my shoe out and carefully unhooked his claws from the lace. '*Bad* cat!'

134

He rolled on his back and made a grab for my ankle.

'I don't have time to play,' I said. 'I've got things to do. I'll play with you when I get home.'

I ran downstairs. Amanda was sitting in the hall waiting for me.

'About time!' she said. 'I've been waiting for ten minutes down here. As if it isn't bad enough that I've got to take you in the first place.'

'Calm down,' I said. 'I'm ready now.'

We said goodbye to Mom and headed off for the rink.

'What were you talking to Pippa about a lunch?' I asked, trying to sound real casual about it.

'Huh?' Amanda said. 'Oh, that. She was just asking what I had planned for the weekend.'

'Is that all?'

'Sure. Why?'

'I just wondered,' I said. 'What did you tell her?'

Amanda looked suspiciously at me. 'What's going on?' She said. 'Why are you and your nerdy friends suddenly so incredibly interested in whatever I do?'

'Beats me,' I said.

'If you think you're going to tag along with

me over the weekend, you can forget it,'
Amanda said. 'I've got plans. And they don't
involve my kid sister and her little buddies,
OK?'

'What makes you think we'd want to follow
you around all weekend?' I said.

'I don't know,' Amanda said. 'But you were
sure determined to get me to take you skating
this evening.' She gave me a sharp look. 'And
don't think I don't know what you were trying
to do.'

'What's that supposed to mean?' I asked.
This was a real shock. Had Amanda figured
it out?

'Asking me to take you skating in front of
Mom,' Amanda said. 'You knew she'd make
sure I *did*.'

Phew! She had me worried for a moment
there. I thought for a second that she really
had figured out what we were up to.

I smiled at her. 'You should be flattered that
I would *want* you to teach me how to skate
backward,' I said.

'Yeah, sure,' Amanda said. 'I'm totally flattered, Stacy.'

'You never know,' I said with a grin. 'You
might end up having a great time.'

I had my fingers crossed behind my back.

Come on, Jake, I was thinking. *Don't let me down, now. You be there!*

He was there, OK. But that was just the *start* of it!

14

The Paradice rink was part of a big sports centre in the middle of town. When we arrived, there were quite a few people zooming around on the ice, as well as the usual collection of learners tottering around on their skates and clinging to the barrier.

I sat on a bench by one of the entrances to the ice and put on the skates I'd rented.

Amanda went out on to the ice and did a real flashy turn before coming back to the entrance. 'Come on,' she said. 'Are you going to sit there all night?'

I teetered out on to the ice, holding on to the barrier.

Why did I do this? I thought, remembering all the bruises I'd gone home with last time I'd tried skating backward.

I let go of the barrier. I skate pretty well as long as I only try to go forward. It's all the twists and twirls that I can't handle.

Amanda did a pirouette and sailed past me

with one leg in the air and a huge grin on her face. 'Try that,' she said. 'It's all a question of balance.'

It's all a question of falling flat on my face, I thought.

'No laughing at me!' I said.

'I won't laugh,' Amanda said. 'Give me your hand.'

I grabbed on to Amanda's hand and she towed me along. I tried lifting one leg out behind me the way Amanda was doing.

'Lean forward,' Amanda said.

I leaned. *Oowowwp!* I nearly overbalanced. I grabbed at Amanda.

She started laughing.

'You said you wouldn't laugh!' I said.

'I didn't know you were going to be so funny,' Amanda said. 'Do you want to try going backward now?'

I looked around in the hope that Jake might already be there. There was no sign of him. *Thanks, Jake – my backside and I are going to have a really good time if you don't turn up pretty soon.*

Amanda kicked off and did a perfect backward circle around me.

'And that's all there is to it,' she said. 'All you need is a little confidence.' Yeah, a little confidence and a big cushion strapped to my rear end.

'I'll be right behind you,' Amanda said. 'You just push forward with your lead skate.'

I straightened up, spreading my arms for balance. I kicked off and sailed backward toward Amanda with my arms windmilling.

'That's just fine,' Amanda said. 'Now keep the momentum going. And watch where you're going!'

Someone went whistling past and I nearly jumped out of my boots.

'It's OK,' Amanda said. 'No one's going to bump you. Have a little faith in yourself, Stacy.'

'That's easy for *you* to say,' I said. But I did what she said. I ignored the guys as they sailed past, and did my best to believe that I wasn't going to end up in a heap on the ice. Amanda glided around me as I slid backward over the ice.

'Hey!' I said. 'I'm doing it!'

'Sure you are,' said Amanda. 'Now try it a little faster.'

I was doing real well when someone came crashing into me from behind and I found myself flat on my face with someone lying on top of me.

Except that it wasn't just one person. It was

two: two seven-year-old people, laughing and yelling as they picked themselves up.

I sat up. 'You idiots!' I said, looking up at Denny and Bob's grinning faces.

'You should keep out of the way,' said Denny. (Or it might have been Bob – they're identical twins and not many people can tell them apart.)

'What a goofball!' said Bob (or it might have been Denny).

Before I could think of a satisfactory reply, they'd skated off.

Amanda came sailing over and helped me to my feet. 'You OK?'

'I'm fine!' I said. 'Can we try something else?'

'OK,' Amanda said. 'Let's try a little speed.'

She held on to my hand and we headed off around the ice, Amanda towing me along as I skated like mad to keep up with her.

If Denny and Bob were there, I knew Cindy had to be somewhere. I looked around for her and almost fell over again.

'Concentrate, Stacy,' Amanda said. 'Watch what you're doing, for heaven's sake.'

We did a half-circle of the ice.

'That's more like it,' Amanda said. 'You're getting better. How about some real speed, now?'

We skated past one of the entrances and I saw Jake standing there.

'Hi, Amanda,' he called. 'I got your – '

Amanda towed me straight past. She didn't even *see* him.

'Hey, Amanda,' I said, 'wasn't that – *whoop!*' My skates slid out from under me and I landed on my behind.

Jake had come out on to the ice and was following us. He did a sidesweep to avoid me and crashed right into Amanda.

Next thing I knew they were both sprawling on the ice.

'You clumsy idiot!' Amanda yelled at him. 'Can't you watch where you're going!'

She picked herself up and gave Jake an angry stare as she hoisted me up on to my feet. 'Keep away from us!' she said, towing me away while Jake was still getting to his feet.

I managed a quick glance back at Jake. He looked kind of puzzled. I began to feel this whole business was going to be a lot more complicated than I'd expected.

The next thing that nearly had me flat on my back was when I saw Pippa and Fern peeping out from behind the barrier. I could only see their eyes and noses. They looked like they were trying to keep out of sight. But what the heck were they doing there?

'Stand up *straight*!' Amanda said. I looked around as we slid past Pippa and Fern, but they'd ducked down behind the barrier and I couldn't see them any more.

'Hey,' I said. 'There's Cindy!' I'd finally caught sight of her, over on the far side of the rink. She was doing real neat figure-eights around Denny and Bob. She was supposed to be nearby, pretending to bump into me so that I could go into my twisted ankle routine. 'Let's go say hello,' I said to Amanda.

'We'll keep away from those brats,' Amanda said, pulling me into an area where there were no other skaters. 'OK,' she said, 'let's fly!'

That was when I had my *next* big shock of the evening. Brad Schnieder was out on the ice! He was skating straight toward us.

'This way,' I said, pointing away from Brad.

'OK,' Amanda said. 'Hang on to your hair, Stacy!'

We went skimming around the curve, Amanda keeping hold of my hand as I zipped along in her wake, just managing to keep my balance.

'Is this fun?' Amanda yelled back at me.

Fun? Faces whipped by as we rounded the curve of the rink at top speed. 'How am I going to stop? I can't stop. . . . He-e-elp!'

143

'Keep your feet straight,' Amanda yelled. 'I'm going to let go!'

'No-o-o-o!' I wailed, as Amanda let go of my hand and I went careering on with my arms waving.

I was saved by Cindy. She came speeding up and caught hold of my arm. I went flying round her about three times before my skates slid out from under me and I came to a freezing stop on my backside.

'Wow!' Cindy said, helping me to my feet. 'That was *impressive*, Stacy.'

'You're supposed to be helping me,' I panted, as I hung on to her. 'What happened to the plan?'

'I was just coming over,' Cindy said.

'I saw Brad Schnieder!'

'What? Where?' Cindy said.

'Over *there*!' I gasped. 'And Fern and Pippa are here, too! Don't you see what's happened? Amanda must have told Pippa she was going to be here tonight! Fern and Pippa must have planned to have Brad meet Amanda here!'

'What about Jake?' Cindy asked. 'Have you seen *him*?'

'I'll say. He crashed right into Amanda. She called him an idiot.'

'What are we going to do?' Cindy asked.

144

'We've got to keep Brad away from Amanda,' I said.

Amanda came skating over to us. 'You OK, Stacy?' she asked.

'Yeah! No thanks to you!' I hollered. 'Why did you let go of me?'

'I thought you'd be OK,' Amanda said with a grin. 'You were really speeding along there! Do you want to try it again?'

'No, I do not!' I said.

'Uh-oh!' Cindy said in my ear.

I looked around. Brad was heading straight for us.

'Hi, Amanda,' he said. 'I got your note.'

Amanda stared at him. 'What note?'

'The one you left in my locker,' said Brad.

'I didn't leave any note,' Amanda said. *What note?* I was thinking. *Jake is the one with the note.*

I tottered over to Amanda and yanked on her arm. 'Hey, let's speed-skate again,' I said. Anything to get her away from Brad.

'Hi, guys!' Jake came sailing up and did a quick stop in front of Amanda. He smiled at her. 'I got your note,' he said.

'Amanda!' I said in desperation. 'Show me how to speed-skate again, huh?'

'Wait a minute,' Amanda said. She looked

from Brad to Jake. 'What's all this about *notes*?' she said.

'You left me a note in my locker,' Jake said.

'Hold it!' Brad said, staring at Jake. 'She left *me* a note!'

'I did not!' Amanda yelled. 'I didn't leave *anyone* a note!'

'You did,' Jake said, pulling my note out of his pocket. 'Look!'

Amanda grabbed it out of his hand.

'And me!' Brad said, taking out another slip of paper.

Panic time! I let one of my skates shoot out from under me and fell on my rear end on the ice.

'Ow!' I yelled. 'I twisted my ankle!'

Amanda stared at Jake's note. 'That's not my writing,' she said. 'That's Stacy's!'

She looked at Brad. 'Give me that note.'

'Ow! Ow! Ow!' I wailed. 'I think my ankle's *broken*!'

Amanda looked at the two notes. 'And I don't know *whose* writing this is,' she said, 'but it sure isn't mine! What the heck is going on here?' She grabbed hold of my collar and yanked me to my feet. 'Stacy?'

'It wasn't me!' I gasped. 'Honest.'

'You mean you didn't write me a note?' Jake said to Amanda.

'Get it into your head!' Amanda said. 'I didn't write *anyone* a note.' She waved one in Jake's face. 'This one was written by my sister,' she said. 'And *this* one,' she brandished the other at Brad, 'was probably written by one of her nerdy friends!'

'I don't get it,' Brad said. 'Does this mean you didn't want to meet me here?'

Amanda rolled her eyes. 'You catch on quick!' she said.

'It was a mistake,' Cindy said. 'You weren't *both* supposed to get notes.'

Amanda glared at me. 'You set this whole thing up!' she said. 'You and your stupid little pals set me up . . . again! As if once wasn't enough!'

'It wasn't like that,' I said, half-choking in the grip she had on my collar. 'Can we talk about this later? I really hurt my ankle!'

'Forget your ankle!' Amanda exploded. 'I'm going to break every bone in your scrawny body!'

Jake and Brad looked at each other, still trying to unscramble all this.

'Hi, everyone!' We all looked around at this new voice. Cindy's cousin Luke came skating up to us with a big smile on his face.

'Hi, Luke!' Amanda said. She let go of my collar and I went *splat!* on the ice.

'I hope I'm not late,' Luke said, looking straight at Amanda. 'You did say seven-thirty, didn't you?'

'I sure did,' Amanda said with a huge grin. 'And you've arrived at *exactly* the right time.' She stepped over me and linked arms with Luke. She looked down at me. 'Luke and I are going to do some skating,' she said. 'I'll leave you to explain everything to these two.'

'Yeah, but – '

Amanda didn't hang about. I watched in total amazement as she and Luke went sailing off across the ice.

'What is going on here?' Jake said.

'Oh – ' Cindy said. 'I think I'd better go see how Denny and Bob are doing.' She skated off as well. Thanks, Cindy. Big help!

I looked up at Jake and Brad. 'I can explain,' I said. 'Uh – you see – Amanda fell out of her cot when she was a baby. She landed right on her head and she's been having these weird memory blackouts ever since.'

'You are one strange family,' Brad said, shaking his head.

'Let's get out of here,' Jake said. They skated off, leaving me sitting there on the ice all on my own.

Well! That's absolutely the last time I'm ever going to do Amanda any favours with boys! Talk about a total disaster: all I ended up with was a whole bunch of bruises and a freezing behind.

15

'Why didn't you tell us what you were planning?' I asked. Pippa and Fern just looked at me.

'Why didn't you tell *us*?' Fern replied.

The four of us were sitting in the spectators' area behind the barrier. Every now and then Amanda and Luke would come skating past, looking like they were having a great time together.

'We thought of it first,' I said.

'How were we supposed to know that?' Pippa said. 'And, anyway, how do you know you thought of it first? *We* might have.'

'Guys,' Cindy said, 'I don't think it really matters who thought of it first.' Amanda and Luke went sweeping past, looking just like my vision of how this evening was supposed to go. Except that Amanda's brilliant partner was Luke instead of Jake.

'It looks to me like Amanda had her own ideas, anyhow,' Cindy said.

'I'll say,' Fern said. She grinned. 'I guess she made us all look like dummies.'

'When did you put the note in Brad's locker?' I asked.

'This afternoon,' Pippa said.

Sheesh! It was a good thing Brad and Jake had lockers in different hallways, or we'd have bumped into each other!

'What did you say to Brad to get him to call Amanda?' Cindy asked.

'He called?' Pippa said. She looked at Fern. 'See? I told you he'd call her.'

'Wait a minute,' Fern said. 'How did *you* know he'd called? Did Amanda say something?'

'No,' Cindy said. 'Stacy answered the phone. She hid the message so Amanda wouldn't find it.'

'Thanks, Cindy,' I said. 'Thanks for telling them.'

'You big cheat!' Pippa said. 'And you were accusing me of cheating! If Amanda had gotten that call, Brad would have asked her out.'

'OK, I'm sorry,' I said. 'But I'm not so sure she'd have agreed to go out with him anyway. Take a look out there – she's not interested in Jake *or* Brad.'

151

'She sure looks interested in Luke, though,' Fern said.

'They must have fixed this up when Amanda brought his jeans back,' Cindy said. 'Wow! Amanda and Luke.'

'I know,' I said. 'And after all our *work*!'

'I guess we wasted our time,' Pippa said. 'It looks like your sister can run her own love-life.'

'Let's not do anything like this again, huh, guys?' Cindy said. 'Let's just forget the whole thing.'

I went along with that. It was too much of a strain.

THE GREAT MATCHMAKING
COMPETITION: FINAL SCORE

Stacy and Cindy – zero!

Pippa and Fern – zero!

Amanda – game, set and match!

★ ★ ★

Luke came back to our house on the bus that night. I sat on the seat behind while Luke and Amanda talked endlessly. Amanda was definitely ignoring me. Every now and then Luke would lean over the seat and say something to me, but I hardly got a word out of Amanda the entire trip.

I left the two of them gabbing on the doorstep. I kept track of the time. They were out there for a full half-hour before I heard the door close.

I expected Amanda to come and yell at me, but she didn't. She seemed to be in a terrific mood. I could hear her singing to herself in her bedroom.

'You know what?' I said to Benjamin, who was lying dozing on my bed. 'I think I'm going to get away with this. Amanda's in too good a mood to yell at me.'

A little later I bumped into Amanda in the hall on my way to the bathroom. She had a grin that went from ear to ear.

'Are you mad at me?' I asked.

'Me?' Amanda said, still grinning. 'Now why should I be mad at you, Stacy? You're the one who came out of this looking like a total idiot!' She laughed. 'Did you really think I wouldn't find out? I mean, come *on*, Stacy – trying to set me up with *two* dates at once?'

'That wasn't the plan at all,' I told her. 'Cindy and I wrote the note to Jake, but it was Pippa and Fern who wrote the note to Brad Schnieder. I didn't know anything about it.'

Amanda shook her head. 'What made you

153

think I'd want a date with *either* of them?' she asked.

'You said you wanted to meet some interesting boys,' I said.

'I never did,' Amanda said. 'I never said anything of the sort.'

'You *did*,' I said. 'I read it in your – ' I bit my tongue. Rats! Now I was going to be in trouble.

'You read my diary!' Amanda exploded. 'You sneaked into my room and read my *private* diary!'

'Not on purpose,' I said. 'It was lying open in there. I only went in there to borrow your magic markers. Do you think I'd read it on purpose?'

'I'm going to keep my room locked from now on,' Amanda said. 'I'm not having nosey little kids creeping in there whenever they feel like it!'

'I wasn't being nosey,' I said. 'Sheesh! I was trying to do you a favour, Amanda.'

'When I need your help, I'll ask for it,' Amanda said. 'And what makes you think I'd go out with a boy *you* picked? You don't understand the first thing about boys!' She flounced back to her room.

I'll tell you what I didn't understand. I didn't understand why someone as nice as

Luke would want to spend any time with a bimbo like Amanda. *That*'s what I didn't understand.

★ ★ ★

Next morning I was eating breakfast with Mom, Dad and Sam, when Amanda came downstairs. She was already dressed. Most Saturdays she isn't even out of bed before mid-morning.

'Did you have a nice time last night?' Dad asked.

'Sure did,' Amanda said. I was expecting her to blab about what had happened. Amanda *loves* to make me look dumb in front of Mom and Dad. 'Would you believe I had *three* dates?' she said.

I bit into my peanut-butter toast. That's it, Amanda, humiliate me!

'Three dates?' Dad said. 'How did you manage that?'

'Oh, with a little help from Stacy and her friends,' Amanda said. 'You know how we just love helping each other.' I looked up. Amanda was smiling. 'In fact,' she continued, 'Stacy's been so helpful to me recently, that I'm going to have to make a real effort to even things up between us.'

Uh-oh! I didn't like the sound of that.

Whatever Amanda was cooking up, I was pretty sure I wasn't going to like it.

Amanda ate a quick breakfast. 'I'm going over to the Spiegels' house,' she said. 'I promised to say goodbye to Luke. They're leaving for South Bend around noon. As soon as they get there, he's going to give me a call. He says there's a bus that goes between here and South Bend, so he'll be able to come visit sometimes.'

'That's nice,' Mom said.

'It sure is,' Amanda said. 'He's great. We get along real well.' She gave me a look. 'He's a very interesting person. Not like all the other guys around here.'

'I can see we're going to have to keep an eye on the phone bill from now on,' Dad said with a smile. 'Plenty of calls to South Bend, huh?'

'I hope so,' Amanda said. 'OK. I'm off now.' She gave me another look. 'I've just got one quick visit to make first. See you guys later.'

Now why had she looked at *me* when she'd said that? It didn't take a genius to figure that Amanda was up to something.

I found out what the *something* was later that afternoon. The doorbell rang around four o'clock and Mom called upstairs to say that it was someone for me.

'I'm really pleased you changed your mind,' Mom said softly, as I came down the stairs. 'I know you didn't want to go at first.'

Huh? What was she talking about?

She patted me on the head. 'You're a good girl, Stacy,' she said, and walked into the kitchen.

I went to the door.

Davey Brown was standing there. 'Hi,' he said. 'I'm here.'

I gave him a puzzled look. I could *see* he was there. What did he want this time? Wasn't he *ever* going to give up trying to make friends with me?

'I got your note,' he said. 'I'm real glad you were able to cancel the other things you had planned for this afternoon. Everything's ready. You can come over right away.'

'What note?' I asked.

He smiled and showed me a slip of paper. I took it from him: *Dear Davey. I'm not going to be busy this afternoon after all, so I'd love to come to your party. Come over to my house when the party starts. I'm really looking forward to it. Stacy.*

It was in Amanda's handwriting.

'You *did* write it, didn't you?' Davey said, with a sudden worried look.

I smiled at him. 'Sure I did,' I said. What

else could I say? Amanda had set me up well. She'd sure paid me back for trying to meddle in *her* life.

It wasn't so bad, though. Davey Brown wasn't such a nerd once you got to know him. And those rabbits of his were the cutest things you've ever seen.

But I'll tell you one thing – that was the very *last* time I was ever going to get involved in trying to find a boyfriend for my big sister Amanda. She can sort out her *own* dates from now on!

Stacy and Amanda are back in **Little Sister Book 4**, *Copycat*, coming soon from Red Fox. Here's a sneak preview:

Chapter One

'Hi, folks. I'm Stupendous Stacy Superstar, and I'd like to welcome you to another episode of this network's most popular family show, *I-I-I Don't Belie-e-e-eve It*! Yeeeeeah!' I flashed a big game-show-host grin and Cindy went: 'Brrrrm – *chissssh*!' (Drum-roll and cymbal clash).

The audience went Wild.

'Woo! Yeah! Yo! Yee-haah!' The audience consisted of my three best friends and was taking place in my bedroom. I'm Stacy Allen, *aka* Stupendous Stacy Superstar, game-show host extraordinaire.

I held my hands up to try and quiet down the rowdier elements in the audience. (Fern makes a really good rowdy element).

'And our first contestant on *I Don't Believe*

Oooh, Stacy and the gang really do get themselves into some tricky situations. Check out book six for more fabulous fixes. Here's a taster to get you on your way.

The New Guy

1

I think my mon has a new boyfriend.

I haven't met him yet. I've only seen a picture of him so far, but Mom's invited him for dinner at our house next Saturday. And the question that's worrying me is this: what's going to happen next if the dinner is a raging success?

He's a colleague of Mom's – in the staff faculty at the college where my mon works. She's a professor. Professor Elizabeth Kane. That's my mom. Pippa Kane – that's me. My mom is the smartest mom in the known Universe. (She's probably the smartest mom in the unknown parts of the Universe, too – but, hey, how's a person to know?)

My mom's new boyfriend has a beard and his name is Kevin Strink.

A beard I could maybe cope with.

A guy called Kevin Strink I could maybe

deal with – even though it's already kind of difficult not to think of him as Kevin Stink.

But both together??

Can you imagine?

Well, actually, you don't have to imagine – 'cos I'm going to tell you about it.

It all began one dark and stormy night. The owls were hooting in the distant trees and the full moon was staring down from out of a black and featureless sky. Hideous deformed monsters were lumbering and shuffling through people's backyards – searching for any living being foolish enough to venture out of doors.

At least, that's what was happening according to my pal Stacy.

We were having a slumber party at Stacy's house.

By 'We' I mean me and my three best friends: Fern Kipsak, Cindy Spiegel and Stacy Allen. Our gang is just like the Three Musketeers – All For One And One For All. Like in the film, yeah? Except that there are four of us. There are four guys in the film, too – I guess someone along the line there was really bad at math.

When we have slumber parties, we always seem to wind up telling one another spook stories.

'And then the vampire librarian dragged the bleeding bodies away from the Horror section in the library, and down into that dank, dark, deadly, secret dungeon,' Stacy intoned in a deep, sinister voice. She had a really great flashlight that had three different coloured filters over the front – so you could have a blue light, or a red or green one. Right then Stacy had a red light because of all the blood that the vampire librarian had sucked. 'And from that day to this, George and Matilda Snookpoodle were never seen again,' Stacy finished. 'Hurr, hurr, hurrrrghhh!' (Gruesome laugh.)

'Huh!' said fern. 'That wasn't scary.'

'Yes it was,' said Cindy from Stacy's closet. 'I'm never going to the library again. I knew there was something strange about the librarian woman.' When things start to get creepy, Cindy always goes and sits in the bottom of Stacy's closet with the door closed. She says it makes her feel more secure.

Cindy's the kind of girl who would throw the sheets up over her head if she woke up and found a werewolf in her bedroom. You know the type of person: they'd hide away under the bedcovers and hope the werewolf would go away. Personally, I'd try to engage it in pleasant conversation until it calmed down, 'cos it's a Well-Known Fact that once a werewolf calms down, it turns back into a regular person and quits trying to kill you.

Fern says she'd blast it with her intergalactic blaster-ray.

'There's no such thing as intergalactic blaster-rays!' Stacy told her.

'Oh, right,' said Fern. 'Like there are a whole mess of real werewolves! Not!'

Fern started telling us a story about these huge, invading space-octopuses from a distant galaxy.

She shone the flashlight up into her face. On green.

'And the monster octopuses from Saturn landed outside town in the middle of the night –' Fern began.

'Excuse me,' I whispered. 'I thought you said they were from a distant galaxy.'

'They are,' Fern said crossly, annoyed at being interrupted. 'A very distant galaxy. What of it?'

'Saturn isn't in a distant galaxy.' I reminded her. 'Saturn is in our galaxy.' Thing is, when your mom's a college professor, and you're the kind of person who likes to read books and find stuff out, you wind up knowing interesting things like where Saturn is. 'Saturn is a planet in our solar system,' I continued. 'It's the one with the rings.' Fern glared at me. 'Actually, it's the second largest planet in the solar system,' I explained helpfully. 'It has an atmosphere composed mostly of –'

'Pippa?' Fern growled.

'Yuh?'

'If you say one more word, I'm gonna kill you.'

Fern is my very best friend. I thought I ought to mention that at this moment, just in case you're worried that she might have meant that about killing me. Fern says stuff like that when she's mad. She doesn't mean it. She's always threatening to kill, pulverise, mash, stomp and spifflicate people if they get her mad. Underneath, Fern's a real pussycat. She hardly ever really kills people. Except when there's a full moon. (Only kidding.)

'OK,' I said. 'I can take a hint.'

'Good,' said Fern. She stared at me, her face all green and gruesome in the green and gruesome light. 'So, these space-octopuses, like, landed from their home planet of Saturn, which is an entirely different Saturn from the one Pippa was just talking about. And it's in a totally different galaxy to ours. Twenty squillion miles away, in fact! It just happens to have the same name as that planet

Pippa was talking about, right?' She glared at me. 'Got that?'

'Got it,' I said. 'That explains everything.' I thought it was kind of strange that two planets should both be called Saturn, but I decided not to mention this to fern.

'And after they had landed, the space-octopuses used their six tentacles like propeller blades to screw themselves into the ground.'

'Eight tentacles,' I said softly.

'And they screwed themselves right into the ground until only their eyes were showing,' Fern said.

'It's eight tentacles, actually,' I muttered.

'And then, the next morning, when a school bus came past, one giant space-octopus jumped out of the hole and wound its tentacles right around the bus.'

'I think you'll find it's eight,' I said quietly.

Fern turned on me. 'What the heck are you muttering about?' she yelled.

'Octopuses have eight tentacles,' I said.

'She's right,' Stacy said, nodding. 'And I think a whole bunch of octopuses are called octopi.' Stacy knows heaps of stuff about animals. She's really into wildlife and nature and stuff like that. She has a big poster of a tiger on her bedroom wall.

'Space-octopuses from the other Saturn only have six tentacles,' yelled Fern.

'And a bunch of them is called octopuses! Got it?'

'Got it,' Stacy and I said in chorus.

'Octopi!' Fern grumbled. 'What kind of a word is that? It sounds like something they'd serve in the cafeteria on a really bad day.' She shone the green light up onto herself again. 'If I might be allowed to continue with my really interesting story . . .' she said. 'What happened next was that the space-octopus wiggled its tentacles in through the windows of the school bus. Then it started to pluck the kids out one by one, and stuff 'em into its big hungry mouth.' Fern grinned fiendishly. 'The kids would go pop as they came out through the windows and cru-u-urnch when the space octopus chomped down on 'em.'

'I need to go to the bathroom,' Cindy said from the closet. She crawled out and went over to the door on all fours. She peered into the hall.

'It's OK,' Stacy said with a laugh. 'The only kind of monster you'll find out there is called the Dreadful Brainless Amando-saurus.'

She meant her big sister, Amanda.

I've often wondered what it would be like

to have a sister. Sometimes I think I might have liked it – not that it's going to happen now. Mom and Dad split up two years ago. I was totally devastated at the time, but after a while I almost got used to it, you know? Life goes on, I guess, and you have to kind of put the really miserable stuff behind you.

Actually, my mom came up with a good idea for getting rid of miserable stuff. You close your eyes and imagine a note-pad. Then you imagine a pencil. Then you write with the imaginary pencil on the imaginary note-pad. You write down all the details of whatever's bugging you or upsetting you or whatever. Then you put the note-pad into a big imaginary envelope. Then you address it to Asfarawayaspossible, Northern Alaska. Then you mail it. And then it's gone.

I think a lot about how things were when we were a family, but towards the end it seemed like Mom and Dad were arguing all the time, so I guess it was better for them to live apart. Dad lives in New Mexico now, which is a long way from the town of Four Corners, Indiana, where I live with my mom. Just the two of us. On our own.

Except that if Mom does decide she wants Stinky Kevin for her boyfriend, I have the bad feeling that things are going to change. I don't like the idea of things changing. I kind of like things the way they are.

Anyway, Cindy came back from the bathroom and Fern carried on with her story. It kind of ran out of steam after the giant space-octopuses had eaten everyone on the planet.

Then it was my turn. I took the flash-light from fern and turned the revolving coloured thing on to blue. 'This is the story,' I moaned, 'of the dreadful, fiendish thing that Amanda Allen constructed in her basement. I call this gut-wrenching little tale "Franken-boyfriend!"'

Then I told them the tale of how Amanda sneaked stuff home from the school bio labs: little shreds of chopped-up bodies. And how she hung around graveyards and landfill sites, collecting all the grizzly items she needed to build herself the perfect boyfriend.

'That's the only way she'd ever get a boyfriend to suit her,' Stacy said. She laughed. 'And the most important thing would be to leave the skull totally empty. If she gave Frankenboyfriend even a tiny weenie little brain, it would realise what an airhead she is.'

Sometimes Stacy and Amanda seem to get along fine, but for a whole lot of the time, it's like they have real trouble living under the same roof without murdering one another.

Somehow my monster story got derailed and we started to discuss Amanda Allen's Perfect Boyfriend.

How to describe Amanda Allen? Well – I guess Stacy's description is as good as it gets.

'Amanda is a big, dumb airhead Bimbo without a brain. She likes cheerleading, watching TV, blabbing on the phone with her Bimbo friends, hanging around the mall, buying trendy clothes, looking in the mirror and talking about boys. And nothing else. If she was twice as smart as she actually is, she still wouldn't be a half – wit! Uh . . . but sometimes she's an OK person, underneath it all.

I guess that just about covers it.

In the end we decided that Amanda's Perfect Boyfriend would be a tree trunk with a baseball cap on one end, a big wallet in its back pocket, and a fast car to drive her around town in. A really, really dumb tree trunk.

All this talk of boyfriends set me to thinking.

'Guys,' I said. 'I have something to tell you.'

They all looked at me.

'I don't know if this is something I should be worrying about, or not,' I told them.

'Uh-huh?' said Stacy.

'I don't even know it it's really gonna happen,' I added.

'OK,' said Cindy.

'I might be getting jumpy over nothing,' I said.

'Are you going to tell us, or what?' said Fern.

I blinked at her. 'I think . . .' I began.

'Yeah?' they all said, leaning expectantly towards me.

'I think . . .' I said again, 'and I could be wrong . . .'

'Get on with it!' Fern howled.

'I think my mom has a new boyfriend!' I wailed. 'His name is Kevin and he has a beard and he works with my mom and Mom's invited him over for dinner next Saturday night and I don't know what's going to happen if they get together and really like each other and decide to get married and live in the same place 'cos he lives in Mayville and I don't want to move away from you guys and it's go be really weird if he wants to move in with us because I really like the way things are right now with Mom and me and I don't want some geek turning up and ruining

everything!'
    There! I'd said it!

And there's more . . .

Stacy and Friends 3

My Sister, My Slave

When Amanda starts to become a school slacker, Mom is ready to take drastic action – pull Amanda out of the cheerleading squad! So the sisters make a deal; Stacy will help Amanda with her school work in return for two whole days of slavery. But Amanda doesn't realize that when her little sister's boss, two days means 48 *whole* hours of chores – snea-kee!

ISBN 0099263599 £3.50

Stacy and Friends 4

My Real
Best Friend

It's show time! TV stardom beckons
with a slot on the infamous 'Best of
Friends' game show. Cindy and Stacy
are a winning team, until Stacy does
something sneaky and they stop
speaking to each other! Then Pippa
and Fern have a fall-out too! Suddenly,
it's time to regroup and find a *new* best
friend. And while they're all working
flat out to find out as much as they
possibly can about each other, they
end up finding out a whole lot about
themselves too . . .!!

ISBN 0099263629 £3.50